# Thistle
# in the
# Long
# Grass

# Thistle in the Long Grass

## E. I. Parr

The Book Guild Ltd

First published in Great Britain in 2023 by
The Book Guild Ltd
Unit E2 Airfield Business Park,
Harrison Road, Market Harborough,
Leicestershire. LE16 7UL
Tel: 0116 2792299
www.bookguild.co.uk
Email: info@bookguild.co.uk
Twitter: @bookguild

Typeset in 11pt Minion Pro

rinted and bound in Great Britain by CMP UK


ISBN 978 1915352 651


British Library Cataloguing in Publication Data.
A catalogue record for this book is available from the British Library.

Kath,

Best Wishes,

Liz

( E.l.Parr )

# 1

# Playing with Toys: Summer 1965

THE REFLECTION IN a floor-length, teak hall mirror stared back at her. It was a little girl with ice-blonde curls, wearing a simple-cut, short-sleeved, mint-green dress emblazoned with poppies. The girl's eyes widened in disbelief and, brimming with tears, held her gaze, but only for a moment. Karen decisively grabbed the front-door handle and made her escape. Running as fast as her eight-year-old legs would allow, she sped along the cul-de-sac, turning sharply left into the road on which her home stood one quarter of a mile down the hill. Her chest pounding and her breath laboured, she arrived at the front gate. Her feet screeched to a halt. Looking at the neat, three-bed, semi-detached, pebble-dash house a thought crashed through her child's understanding: 'I must *not* tell them.' In that moment her fearful, crystal-blue eyes noticed a tall weed growing from a hardly visible patch of soil between the pavement and garden wall. At the top of its slender stem was poised a deep purple flower. Such a naturally pretty sight, except the flower-head was surrounded by ugly, sharp barbs curling inwards as if to prevent anyone from plucking the bloom. She wanted to pick the flower-head – for comfort, but her finger was pricked by one of its spikes. Stifling a cry, she ran down the concrete drive and around to the back door. The door was open. Inside, Mother, a pint-sized woman with overly lacquered, back-combed brunette hair, was attempting to flay her arms as a tall, muscular man, Father, gripped her wrists. Voices laced with familiar anger and recognisable screams of terror filled the kitchen. Mother noticed a silent Karen. "Karen – run up the road – quickly… see if the policeman at number forty-three is home." Once again Karen found herself in a state of panic. The policeman's wife sat her on a wicker kitchen chair and offered the sobbing child a glass of lemonade. Karen declined. Her stomach was heaving, and her body bent almost double. She focussed on her scuffed, red summer sandals. In suppressing the urge to vomit she swallowed every gulp of emotion that unmercifully rose in her throat.

Father had left the house when Karen returned home. Mother said nothing; neither did Karen. A few weeks later a plump lady wearing a pink crimplene skirt-suit came to the door. Mother guided this stranger into the front room, which was sparsely furnished, the standout piece of furniture being a proud, mahogany-veneered piano.

"Hello, Karen. My name is Miss Ramsey. I expect you are old enough to understand that there has been a big change in your life."

"When is Daddy coming home?" asked Karen, knowing that the 'big change' would have been obvious to a child of any age.

"Well – I am afraid that is the difficulty, Karen. You see – it may not be for a very long time. So, your mother feels that it would be much better for you to live somewhere that is more like a normal family, just for a while."

Mother would not catch Karen's enquiring expression.

Miss Ramsey cast a fishing line: "Wouldn't it be fun to be with other children, in a place where people do not argue?"

Karen pictured a happy house, filled with merriment and laughter. This visualisation had appeal to an 'only' child, accustomed to witnessing domestic abuse.

"Will there be a piano?" Karen eyed her stately, looming friend whose ivory keys seemed to be winking at her.

"I am sure there will be." Miss Ramsey's hand was fleshy and damp as she held Karen's, leading her away from the house. The thistle was even taller now. Karen let go of podgy fingers to pause in appreciation of this delicate, ferociously safeguarded floret. "Goodbye, thistle." Mother remained in the pebble-dash edifice.

Chantry House was situated in the corner of a dead-end close on the periphery of a post-war council housing estate. It was of typical red-brick design, L-shaped with large windows. The garden surrounding the property was laid to lawn and littered with cheap plastic toys. There were several sounds emanating from this avocado junkyard; only some could be described as 'laughter'. Karen felt an urge to turn tail and run but it was too late. Another sweaty palm seized her own as Miss Ramsey waved goodbye. Marshalled through the house, Karen was introduced to a number of rooms, some containing waxy-eyed boys and girls of differing descriptions. Eventually the door was opened into a small bedroom containing four single beds, all neatly adorned with matching coarse, rust-coloured eiderdowns. Karen's suitcase was placed on one bed.

"Put your clothes in this cupboard." The voice pointed towards a floor to ceiling closet. "There are two low shelves bearing your name tag. If you have a favourite doll or cuddly toy it can be placed on the bed. Other toys usually end up shared by everyone – then no-one can become jealous."

Karen took her first peek at the voice. A middle-aged, non-descript woman with greasy hair pulled high upon her head looked down on Karen's curly blonde mop. A stringy body was mostly hidden by a loose-fitting, checked tabard overall; this appeared to be the unofficial care-worker uniform. Karen placed her much loved soft-toy Panda on the pillow indicated.

By night-time Karen had learned that all staff were called 'Miss' irrespective of their marital status. Some appeared kinder than others. Tea was always held at five o'clock. Twelve boys and girls, with ages ranging from five to twelve years, were sat at two steel-legged, melamine-topped tables. The food was wholesome but tasteless. Karen suddenly missed her mother's salty cheese on toast. That first evening melted similarly, like sticky cheese seeping from burned crusts. The hard edge being bath-time. Karen shied away from prying eyes as instructions were issued to undress and climb into a bath of soapy water in which another female child was already sat.

Karen uttered not one word. Having had no siblings, this was a totally excruciating experience. She had seen semi-naked children at school whilst changing for PE, but they always had their knickers on. 'Knickers' – the memory of a missing undergarment filtered through her current predicament and reminded her that absolutely nothing could be as devastating as… then the memory faded; what was it about the knickers? Suddenly she could not recall.

After 'Miss' called out 'Goodnight' and switched off the light, darkened silence pervaded the room, but only briefly. Karen raised her head above the counterpane; a torch was being shone into her eyes. Three faint faces with sneering lips hovered above.

"What's your name then?" rasped the voice of someone older than Karen, whom she recognised as Natalie. The other girls' names Karen could not remember, and Natalie was clearly the bedroom ringleader.

"Thistle…" came a whisper.

"No, it's not," said a different girl. "I heard Miss call you Karen."

"It's Thistle!" Karen found a determined defiance from somewhere inside and fired the name like a poisoned dart towards her roommates.

"You had better do what we say – or 'else' will happen," Natalie boldly retaliated with her own arrows. "Do you know what 'else' is? No – thought not. Well, you really don't want 'else.'"

Karen's eyes were now accustomed to the torchlight. Her piercing pupils stared straight back at Natalie as she offered an authoritative response: "I know all about 'else'.

It holds no fear for me. So – you had better not make any trouble or 'else' will follow you for the rest of your life! And… my name is Thistle."

The girls retreated to their own beds. Karen buried her face in Panda's neck as tears of brine edged their way to her chin. She clasped Panda's right mitt and, like a puppeteer, used it to caress her head. The touch of a straw paw soothed her, and the consoling smell of home hung on Panda like an imperceptible blanket. "Daddy will come and get me soon…" Her faint words escaped through anaglypta-papered walls, in search of the man who had disappeared.

"She's a witch." The children would warily walk past Karen, now known as Thistle, their infantile expressions conveying an irrefutable truth.

"She always gets her own way," one pronounced to another.

"I've seen her ride on a broomstick."

"And that black and white Panda is her 'familiar'," commented an eleven-year-old who had read about such things.

"Yes, why doesn't she have a teddy, like everyone else?"

Thistle retained a calm and composed countenance. Whilst awaiting rescue from her father, she developed her own style of magic, largely by being quietly observant.

She observed the 'Miss' who collected up items of food which had not been dished up, to secrete them away in a holdall. Another 'Miss' always had bitter breath. Thistle found the whisky bottle protruding from her overnight bag. An attractive 'Miss' and the only 'Mr' (the officer-in-charge) would sometimes emerge from his office with dishevelled clothing and beads of sweat trickling from their brows. And then there was 'artful Miss'. She allowed Thistle to bathe alone, as long as 'Miss' was present to soap her back. Thistle did not mind the stroking; it was the only form of human affection she had access to. Her discovery of secrets paved the way to minor power. She did not understand the word 'blackmail'.

The other technique that Thistle found herself applying was to regard adults and children as playthings. Having had no brothers or sisters, and her parents often engaged in varying levels of conflict, back in the family home she had whiled away many hours in two ways. The piano absorbed her completely when parental rancour was dormant and unvoiced, or Father was working. When the bile of her parents' sour relationship spilt out, Thistle would retreat to her bedroom: a refuge in which toys became the only element of her life over which she held any control. Dolls and cuddly animals, including Panda, were arranged to her design, then she would talk on behalf of each one. There was nothing unusual about this common childhood game except that Thistle would encourage antipathy between her charges; one toy would always be seeking dominance over another. When words failed the victim, the aggressor would simply bash the underling until it writhed on the floor. Thistle would pick up the casualty, cradle it and say, "There, there. No harm done. You'll feel better soon, but next time do what you are asked to." These words were copied from those that often floated up the stairs, before Father went

7

missing. *No harm done*, she told herself while playing with the humanoid toys of Chantry House. There was no piano to play (Miss Ramsey had lied about this) and few personal toys to own, so toying with people helped pass the time whilst achieving results. Soon the labels on her shelves and clothing no longer read 'Karen'.

Thistle's new school rather replicated Chantry House: pupils and staff felt compelled to acquiesce to the disarming little girl with blonde curls, sapphire eyes and shrewdness beyond her years. In addition, as the school immediately discovered, the child was bearer of a particular gift. Education could have become more of a challenge had Thistle not, on the first day, come across a piano in the hall. The school piano became conduit for Thistle's selection of charm over blackmail to survive primary education. Having politely asked to sit on its stool, her deft yet stumpy fingers produced a dainty performance rooted in innocence. Nursery rhymes licked the keys, and an echo of virtuousness swirled around the ears of two teachers who had stayed behind after assembly at Thistle's ingenious request. She adeptly displayed her talent for 'playing by ear' alongside a rudimental knowledge of musical notation. A passport to relative freedom from constricts of formal instruction, her skill was utilised at every opportunity. If she did not want to do something there would always be a music-loving teacher taking her under their wing and away from the expectations of others.

"I'm special," she frequently told Panda as she hugged him under the blankets. Elevation to the internal mental state of princess could be attained at any time.

"Where do you live?" asked her first school chum.

"I live in a Bardot's home."

"A what?"

"You know, it belongs to that actress – Brigitte Bardot. That's why it's a Bardot's home." Thistle felt immense dignity to be associated with the renowned icon. Her mispronunciation underpinned how she wished to be perceived.

"So – where is your mother?"

"Oh – she is also an actress, so she travels a lot and visits exciting places."

"Ooaa, aren't you lucky. My mum works down the chippy."

Thistle knew that she was not, in fact, 'lucky' to have an absent mother. Every two weeks a letter would arrive from her, the handwriting and spelling being little better than Thistle's own. A few words, slopped across one sheet of thin paper said nothing worth reading; there was no mention of Daddy or of even a visit. Thistle was encouraged to pen replies which always had to confirm, using the words of a young child, that life was wonderful at Chantry House, everyone was kind and the food was tremendous. She expertly conveyed the staff version of the truth but due to her own tactic of 'gentle persuasion' would be rewarded with a sixpence.

It was early December that Mother appeared in the flesh. She brought a hurriedly wrapped present tied up with tinsel. She also brought a thickset, angular man who wore a khaki uniform. "This is a good friend of mine. I am going to live in Germany with him for a while. Here is your

Christmas present. I am so pleased to know that you love it here. Happy Christmas, Karen."

Thistle took the gift with her head slightly tilted to one side. She did not look directly at her mother's face. This time it was Thistle who was avoiding eye contact. Without uttering a word, she turned and ran off.

"Ungrateful brat," said the man to Mother as they walked back to a car.

Once around the back of the house Thistle threw the present into the bushes. Natalie, having witnessed this, retrieved it and hid it under her own bed in great anticipation of the extra toy which would be hers to open on Christmas day. Thistle had wanted to ask about Father but was deterred by Mother's friend being present. *He will visit me*, she told herself. Every day after school she sat in the dining room, the premium place for watching who came to the front door. One day a boy of similar age pulled up a chair next to her. "I don't care if you are a witch because I am a warlock."

Thistle ignored him.

"My name is Sable."

"Sable is not a name!" Thistle's sense of superiority presided.

"Neither is Thistle a name, so there!" the boy retorted.

"Yes, it is, yes, it is. Oh, go away, you horrid little toad."

"No, I won't. I am waiting for my dad."

"When is he coming?" She was snooping; did this boy have a secret to be discovered?

"Don't know."

"How long have you been waiting?"

"A long time, maybe a hundred years?"

"What about your mother?"

"Dead."

Thistle was not sure that she believed Sable because he couldn't have been waiting for one hundred years, but she and he had something in common, so every day they sat together, waiting and watching. Eventually she wondered if she would have to wait for one hundred years. At Christmas some children received visits, and a few went to relatives. Sable and Thistle still sat in the dining area, now decorated with paper chains. "I saw Father Christmas last year," said Sable.

"He doesn't exist," she replied with spite.

Sable burst into tears and ran away, shouting, "I'm not your friend anymore." After Christmas Sable disappeared. No-one said where he had gone but Thistle was sure that no parent had collected him. He never returned and the template for living in a children's home was evident: children would come and go, as would staff. Relationships of any kind had no solid foundation to support them. Thistle noticed that the harsher staff remained in post longer than their kinder counterparts. Presumably the latter found more congenial employment which did not involve working unsocial hours whilst being bullied by despotic team leaders within an authoritarian system. Thistle had no understanding of the concept of institutionalisation; rules, processes and expected behaviours were inculcated into the fabric of Chantry House, a micro-care establishment that rarely recognised individual choice. Gradually she improved on her three coping mechanisms: manipulation, pretence and withdrawal.

Mother's letters rarely arrived from Germany and the wafer of blue paper made her handwriting harder to decipher. It was nearly eighteen months later when another visit occurred. Thistle saw her mother from the bedroom window. A baby was slung over her shoulder. She managed to wriggle under her bed and refused to come out until Mother had left. Occasionally Thistle would still spend a few days watching from the dining room in hope that Father would appear, but in time that optimism disintegrated. Just before her second Christmas at Chantry House, despite the previous year's proclamation to Sable, she had written to Santa politely requesting that he give her father a lift there on his sleigh.

"...*that is the only present I would like, and I would not have to share Daddy with the others... please, Father Christmas. I am being a good girl...*" These latter words were read aloud to Panda, who understood the child. Daddy's non-appearance confirmed to Thistle that her disbelief in Santa's existence was justified. Something did appear to her, though: the smiley face of Santa began to creep into her dreams, but his smile turned into a snarl and then his mouth opened so wide that she thought he was going to swallow her up. This was her first experience of a nightmare.

The following Yuletide Thistle wrote a letter to the Queen asking her to make enquiries about Father's whereabouts. The 'Miss' on duty gave Thistle an envelope. Having tucked the letter inside, she folded the flap inwards with care, and 'Miss' offered to post it. The letter did not reach the post box; it was crumpled into a ball and aimed with practised precision at the staff-bedroom waste-paper basket. Each day Thistle asked whether the postman had brought her a letter. Surely the kindly Queen would not ignore the earnest pleas of an anguished child. As the weeks passed, Thistle studied the 'Miss' who had purportedly posted her letter. This 'Miss' avoided Thistle, scurrying by with exaggerated industriousness. The refusal to catch Thistle's eye reminded her of Mother on the day Miss Ramsey took Thistle away from home. *That's what guilt looks like*, thought Thistle. She put on her thickest gloves and began to forage in a shady corner of Chantry House's garden. When 'Miss' reached inside her coat pockets for her own winter gloves, her hands tightened their grip on thorny, bunched briar.

As these Christmases came and went Thistle continued with her strategies to both survive and control people and situations, perfecting her skills in readiness for secondary education. Cramming herself into outgrown clothes and retching as she swallowed lumps of leathery liver were amongst general issues of 'children's home' life that had to be addressed; the solution lay with support staff, the 'House Assistants', as they were respectfully referred to. These elderly workers who stitched clothes, assisted at meal-times, sorted laundry, dusted and vacuumed, held no positions of responsibility; however they were key to creature comforts. The sweet little girl with blonde curls and prepossessing sapphire eyes tugged at their heartstrings. She regularly drew them pictures or collected wildflowers for them on her way home from school. In return, better-fitting clothes appeared in her closet, extra bacon replaced inedible innards and chocolate treats appeared under her pillow. Thistle could ensure that her material needs were met, but no amount of favour could meet her hunger for love, that most human and necessary building block of life. She pondered on where her father might be. As there seemed no point in writing letters, she sent out messages from her mind to the man who had deserted her. She would lay perfectly still on her bed and imagine his face, his shock of blond hair, his carved smile. Speaking words that no-one could hear, she begged him to return. The man who had caused her mother to tremble, had demonstrated only love for his flawless daughter. Over time the memory of his face began to fade, until Thistle wondered whether he was just a dream that she once had.

By the time Thistle was eleven she had discovered many secrets about the care staff at Chantry House. She surmised that it would be easy to apply the same formula to secondary school, where she feared that her primary-school charm offensive may wear thin; with such a huge number of teachers it would be impossible to become 'pet' to them all. The local comprehensive school catered for over six hundred pupils, so running errands for staff and hanging around corridors gave Thistle endless opportunities for eavesdropping and relaying her rephrased reiterations for premeditated effect. In addition, she became proficient at making clever use of her fantasies. For example, she convinced many girls that her mother really was a famous actress and one day when they were older, Mother would take them to America, to Hollywood, and introduce them to all their movie heartthrobs. Even those who had their doubts about the truth of this did not question the claim just in case Thistle wasn't lying, and then they would miss out.

Thistle's make-believe world had a vital purpose; it served as a hiding place when she lacked the energy to manoeuvre her way through the battlefield of actuality.

In January 1970 a judicious discussion took place at Thistle's statutory social services case conference. In accordance with the child welfare policy of the time she was not invited to attend. The meeting was comprised of Chantry House residential care staff, a pastoral care representative from secondary school and Thistle's county-appointed social worker.

"Now that we are all up to date on Karen's overall well-being, we must consider what options there are for her in March when she reaches thirteen and has to leave Chantry," lectured the social worker. She continued, "She cannot possibly go to the teenage unit... all those hormonal girls and Karen. Oh no..."

"And by then she would be able to walk up to the local shops on her own, prowl around the park, experiment with all sorts – including boys," commented a senior care worker from Chantry House.

A junior member of the Chantry care staff piped up, "I am not sure that boys will be the problem. She is very self-conscious about her body. When her periods started, she hid for hours. But since attending the school sex-education programme she has taken an interest in the other girls' bodies – almost needing to compare them to her own."

The school's pastoral care delegate was aware of the controversy surrounding 'sex-education lessons' amongst people with prudish beliefs. He felt he should quickly interject: "We at the school find Thistle, using the name she prefers to be called, a most multi-faceted character. She never breaks the rules but has the capability to bend them. I would say she has a talent for it. Then, of course, there are the 'Chinese whispers'; the source is usually traced back to her, and we find that she had her own reasons to start them in the first place. At times Thistle is actually very endearing and people drop their guard, especially when she plays the piano. She is a gifted child and I have noticed that she enters a state of serenity when her attention is fixated on the piano keys. It is hard to believe that she is only twelve – well, now nearly a teenager. Her teachers think she would benefit from an environment in which there would be a willingness to understand her complexities but the minimum of opportunity for theatrical scenarios. And I think she should have regular access to a piano. I believe it is her therapy."

The officer-in-charge of Chantry House considered that his years of experience trumped new-fangled ideas. *Therapy – whatever next?* he thought.

The social worker had recently attended a course: 'Positive Pathways for Children in Care'. She consulted with her line manager. Together they made quick progress.

Thistle may have thought that people were completely blind to her games, but she was mistaken. A few days before her thirteenth birthday a senior care worker explained what was to come next: "As you know, Karen – sorry, Thistle, once thirteen you have to move on from Chantry House. Many young people find being placed in a foster family works well for them."

"In Gloucester, Miss?"

"No, Thistle – why would it be in Gloucester?"

"That's where Doctor Foster went to… in a shower of rain…" Thistle's eyes were twinkling; she had seen this particular 'Miss' outside of Chantry House kissing a man under his umbrella.

"No, Thistle. A foster family are people prepared to act as your parents and we have found an ideal couple who are looking forward to caring for you in their own home. They live near fields on the edge of the city, but you can still attend your school, by bus."

Thistle was not prepared for this announcement. She had heard that at thirteen most females were moved to the 'home for teenage girls'; it was near a shopping precinct and recreation ground. She expected to continue as normal with added forays. Wisely she made no protest.

"Yes, Miss. Thank you, Miss."

It was a drizzly day in mid-March when she was driven to a semi-rural area west of the city. At the end of a narrow, tree-lined lane stood a building that reminded her of the gingerbread house in *Hansel and Gretel*. She had been told that this was a trial period with her new 'family'. Standing at the gate were an ageing couple (Thistle deduced this by their grey hair and slightly stooping frames).

"Thistle… say hello to Mr and Mrs Burridge."

The man held out his hand. "Eric and Vida – pleased to meet you."

Thistle remained mute; there was no sound or sign of other children and she correctly guessed that once more she would be an 'only' child. Her breathing began to quicken;

her mind was racing. She had not experienced panic for an eternity. Then the woman, Vida, took her hand and led her to a bay window.

"Look inside," she said. "We understand that you play extremely well."

Through the glass Thistle was able to scrutinise a chintzy room which housed the largest piano that she had ever seen. A river of emotion began to erode the walls of her cerebral fortress, creating from their sediment a waterfall of weeping.

# 2

# Reasons and Seasons:
# February 1974

THE CASKET DISAPPEARED deep into a man-made fissure. A resting place. Hallowed ground. Thistle watched without a murmur as her heart was wrenched from its cavern to follow the coffin into obscurity. On that murky March morning nearly four years beforehand, she had no premonition of the sanctity, safety and unconditional affection she would find within Eric and Vida's gingerbread house. The endless trees which flanked its borders prevented anyone from looking in; for Thistle this translated as privacy from an invasive, interfering world. But more than that, Eric and Vida, although generations older, never failed to provide her with stimulation, mainly musical but also through their compelling stories of the past, particularly Vida's. Thistle thought of Vida as a brave warrior whose experience of suffering abated her own. Yet Eric and Vida never diminished Thistle's tortured childhood; to have been abandoned by one's parents was a wound to the flesh of human consciousness. They understood the consequences to the development of personality. They had no knowledge of the other trauma in Thistle's history. She could not disclose something which had become the faint rumination of a nightmare she once had, now pushed to the edge of her memory and concealed behind a veil of shame.

"Vida is short for Davida – in Hebrew that means 'beloved.'"

Watching Vida's remains being swallowed by the earth, Thistle thought, *You were my beloved, Vida*. Eric and Vida had become the parents that Thistle hankered for. Now one was dead, and Thistle had been removed from the other.

"A single man cannot foster a girl, especially not one of your age." Social worker words were always about what a person 'could not do', what 'could not happen'.

But everything had happened, and so quickly: Vida's heart attack, the emergency case conference, Eric losing his grip on an inescapable reality. He had liberated Vida when she was thirty-five years old. Even with malnourished features she appeared nearly twenty years younger. Vida had been working as a teacher far from home when the Nazis took her parents and younger siblings. Christian friends of hers found a place in which she could hide out. Thistle read *The Diary of Anne Frank*; it catalogued much of Vida's experience. Eventually she was discovered, but by then her papers had been skilfully altered to show her age as fifteen. Apparently young and strong, she was assigned to manual labour and became one of a relatively small number of prisoners left alive when British Forces entered the camp. She had survived – that was the message she conveyed to Thistle, excluding what Vida decided was unnecessarily distressing detail. Now she was dead. Eric could not liberate her from 'dieses Endziel', 'this final destination'.

On the walls of Eric and Vida's home were tastefully framed photographs of all the young people that they had fostered. Their speciality had been teenagers rather than younger children, and during the almost four years that Thistle lived with Eric and Vida there had been occasional visits from them, now in adulthood. But Thistle believed that she was her foster parents' favourite. It was she who could delight them whilst sat at Eric's baby grand piano. Eric and Vida had a passion for the films of the thirties and forties, plus a collection of vinyl records up to the late 1950s. Thistle became particularly accustomed to the compositions of Jerome Kern, Cole Porter, Irving Berlin and the Gershwins. Her preferred balladeers included Nat King Cole, Frank Sinatra and Peggy Lee.

"Play 'For You, Beloved'… work out 'Dreaming'… how about we sing 'Dancing Days'?" No matter what Eric and Vida requested, Thistle could work it out by ear and they would sing the lyrics: "For you, beloved of my memory, must not stay away too long." Those words fell upon a descending, brittle cocoon in the pewter-grey half-light of a February afternoon, as Thistle said goodbye to her 'beloved'.

Thistle's talent had concreted her relationship with the music teachers at comprehensive school, which in turn provided a further tool for her to control secondary education. Her request for extra music lessons was never refused, achieving the aim to absent herself from a range of other subjects. Teachers of those subjects did not complain; they found her a peculiar pupil who had an armoury of unbelievable tall tales.

"Sorry I am late for school, sir, but I was out with Frank in New York over the weekend and fog caused the flight back to be delayed." Thistle's straight-faced delivery confounded school staff; they were unsure whether she had nerves of steel or had honestly come to believe her own fictions. In any event, her consummate knowledge of the covert aspects of school life was enough to make her an adversary not worth challenging.

One art teacher had no negative thoughts of Thistle. At fifteen she still retained a little 'puppy fat' and he saw her as a ravishing yet enigmatic beauty, the pseudo-origin of Botticelli's Venus. He showed her the famous painting *The Birth of Venus* and asked if she would pose as the deity for him the following Saturday at his friend's studio. In return he would arrange for her to have extra art lessons in place of sports sessions, which he knew she detested. Weekly swimming at the local baths was coming up on her school timetable: the activity she hated the most.

Thistle agreed on the condition that she would not be completely naked; her hair would not have covered her genitals. When she arrived he gave her a length of white voile.

Her unexpected embarrassment of exposing so much of her body was minimised by the narcissism she experienced at playing the gargantuan role of goddess. He was circumspect enough not to lay a hand upon her, but she knew of the gratification he was reaping from admiring her shrouded womanhood. This both thrilled and repulsed her in almost equal measure. Thistle had told Eric and Vida she was going to a schoolfriend's home to work on an English presentation. They asked many questions on her return and the lies became intertwined and intricate. When the art teacher asked her to pose again she said no, but he satisfied himself by watching her with the titillation of knowing what lie beneath her school uniform. Thistle felt his eyes fondling her body and was filled with feelings of repugnance. Her physical matter was no longer her own, so she sought to change it – by losing the puppy fat, losing weight. Eric and Vida assumed her lessened appetite to be a teenage fad.

They had encouraged Thistle to bring friends home for tea. Sometimes this occurred but then it would transpire that the 'friend' had a use. Perhaps they had a collection of comics or magazines that Thistle wanted to acquire, or they had completed a piece of homework which she needed to copy, having not bothered to finish, or even begin, her own. Throughout her time at Chantry House the children had continued to consider Thistle a witch; mud sticks but she did not mind because it ensured their compliance with most of her wishes; they feared being cursed. By the time she reached the 'fourth year' Thistle had decided to hone her fake skills of sorcery. Reading palms and guessing 'star signs' kept her popular (the latter was easy once she had discovered lists of pupils' birthdays in her form teacher's desk drawer). Another ploy was to sketch people's faces, during which time she would add to the clairvoyancy scam with sudden 'visions'. Teenage girls are attracted to drama.

Thistle knew this and played them. Arranging toys was still a pet pastime. This nefarious activity provided a wall, a barrier to meaningful relationships. A mandatory aspect of surviving life was to harvest admiration without forging friendships.

Apart from music Eric and Vida implanted in Thistle an appreciation of being outdoors. Enjoying walks through woods and across fields, she was also happy to assist in the extensive, formally planted garden. These activities were also a successful distraction from study, the outcome being that her only 'O' level passes were in Music and Art. Her CSE Grade 1 English result was taken into account when the careers office helped her find employment as a clerical assistant at the local gas board. She had worked there for three months by February 1974, finding it both stifling to her spirit and corrosive to her sense of self. Her plans to remedy this by gaining control of the work environment were thrown into disarray by Vida's illness and death. No longer did she care what was happening around her in the sprawling open-plan office. Leaving the gingerbread house for a tiny bed-sit on a busy road near the city centre drained her of the verve required for plotting.

"You will like it here; it's in walking distance of your work so that will save you bus money. The upstairs bathroom on the left is the facility that you can use and is not to be confused with the second upstairs bathroom. You will share it with two of the other tenants. I understand that one is a girl about your age… that will be nice for you."

Thistle resisted an urge to bite this social worker's hand as she was led up to the second floor of a once-noble

Edwardian villa now converted into plaster-walled punnets. "I won't like it, and nothing will be 'nice'," she mumbled. The bed-sit's wallpaper was a psychedelic design in a repeated pattern that gave the impression of the room being even smaller than it was. In one corner was a curtained-off section containing a sink, a basic cooker and a few cupboards. In another corner was a built-in, violet-painted wardrobe. Underneath a sash window, edged by mustard-coloured curtains, was a single bed. The only positive feature of the room was a vintage fireplace; the gingerbread house had those. The window looked towards an imposing cross which fronted a church spire. At night it was floodlit. Thistle found this comforting and it proved to be a literal Godsend in March after she had seen *The Exorcist* at the cinema. The nightmares, which usually featured grotesque faces, had continued to plague her, and they became more frequent after she saw the film. There was something about the possessed child that refused to leave her memory. For some time afterwards she had to sleep with the light on, in addition to sharing her bed with Panda. At Eric and Vida's Panda had often been haphazardly dumped in a corner, as indication that a teenager now dwelled within the person of Thistle. At bedtime he would always be lovingly retrieved.

The office manager gave Thistle a half-day off for the funeral. In orthodox Jewish tradition this ritual took place a couple of days after Vida's demise, but the new living arrangements were established ten days beforehand, because Vida had to enter hospital. It was now five o'clock. The event was over. Thistle had attempted to speak with Eric before leaving but one of his relatives whisked him away. An hour later she was sat on a shabby, faux-leather armchair within the four walls of a social services-inspected internment. A tap came at the door; she opened it to a curvaceous girl with ironed-straight, shoulder-length fair hair, dressed in black jeans and a hippy-style tie-dye shirt. "I'm Ruth. You and I share the bathroom this end with that spotty lad at number two. Meant to come round before but had a bit of man trouble… you know."

No, Thistle did not 'know'. Thistle did not care but living alone within this kaleidoscopic container had already become insufferable. She summoned one remaining dreg of energy to greet Ruth pleasantly. 'I must survive' was the mantra chanting through her senses. Ruth proved to be essential in subsisting and invaluable to navigating bed-sit land. She introduced the launderette, the nearest and cosiest pub (one barley wine cost far less than filling the electricity meter for evening warmth), the cheapest second-hand shop and the city's shebeen. Ruth was over a year older than Thistle. Not a social services refugee, just a rebel. It was in the shebeen that Thistle spent her seventeenth birthday. No-one questioned her age in any drinking den, legal or illegal, but in the shebeen alcohol could be augmented by puffing on a shared, pungent, cigar-shaped spliff. Thistle did not enjoy feeling heady and out of control but recognised that survival meant connecting with the inhabitants of this anti-establishment sub-culture, so she inhaled the weed very lightly and learned how to exaggerate the effects. Another distasteful but necessary occurrence were frivolous encounters with young males. Thistle detested their oily hair, bristly chins and odour of patchouli oil, which was used to mask the stench of cannabis. Constantly retaining control, her dalliances were always concluded before intimacy, which inspired some aroused youths to award her a rather unpleasant nickname. But it was with Ruth that she went to see *The Exorcist*; no-one at the cinema asked for identification to prove she was over eighteen. Afterwards she wished they had.

Trying to 'fit in' and therefore command influence became Thistle's foremost objective, and eventually that included the workplace. Being the lowest of the low in terms of clerical assistant was not a natural place of power, but in true Thistle style she set to work enchanting colleagues with a 'little girl lost and impoverished' brand of allure. After she concocted a story about her parents having died in a train crash, they were sympathetic to the waif's plight and would regularly bring her gifts of food and toiletries. One overly concerned lady took a television set around to the bed-sit. Thistle was very grateful but her disdain with the role of office junior began to chafe, as did her other incarnation of 'hippy maid', a character based upon Ruth, which guaranteed continuing peer inclusion. When one is impatient for a new path to appear, it is tempting to take the first trail that one stumbles upon.

It was a humid, sticky Saturday in late August 1974 that Thistle was sat with Ruth and another girl at a bench in the garden of 'Barley Wine pub' consuming Somerset cider. He cruised into the carpark driving a pillar box-red TR6. Ruth and Thistle looked his way – they had seen him and the sports car a few times that summer. His short black hair was neatly sleeked back behind his ears, ebony eyes shone from faintly olive skin and his chin was shaven and scrubbed free of stubble. He always wore a white shirt, unbuttoned to reveal a gold medallion hanging from a hairless chest.

"Ronnie," said the other girl. "His dad has 'fingers in pies' all over the county. Locally he owns a factory making spectacles. Ronnie helps his dad and is obviously well rewarded!" She giggled.

"Girlfriend?" enquired Thistle.

"A few… or more!" Further giggles.

Ronnie nodded an acknowledgement to the girls. Unbeknownst to Thistle he had been carrying out his own surveillance of her. Today, with her flowing, wavy, ice-blonde hair – the curls having grown into a longer, softer style with age – wearing a gypsy cut, frilled cream skirt with a cheesecloth blouse draped over, Thistle was the embodiment of ethereal femininity. His eyes met hers and before long both Ruth and the other girl had made their excuses to leave, being aware of the electricity bounding between the peacock and his intended peahen. The dance of romantic enlightenment began as Thistle delved into Ronnie's situation, past and present, and he responded as if at a job interview.

"I expect you have noticed that I am not completely white?"

*That's quite forward*, thought Thistle, stumped for an answer and not wanting to appear racist. She nodded.

"My grandparents and their families came over from the Punjab in the 1920s. Many Sikhs emigrated to container ports like this one. They were merchants, at first selling stockings and then other items, often door to door. I had relatives who fought for the allies during World War Two. By then they were proud to be accepted as English citizens. Anyway, my mum definitely fell for the English – she met and married my dad!"

Thistle quickly realised that Ronnie's projection of a suave, sophisticated 'young man about town', disguised an unpretentious respect for his kinfolk and an uncomplicated artlessness. *He has no outer casing*, she observed.

Ronnie continued, "I love this city and I'm lucky to be helping Dad with his businesses. Mainly I manage the spectacle factory. I have worked very hard and have my own house now; not bad going for a twenty-seven-year-old. Mum helps in the business too. She doesn't really practise Sikhism anymore, but she does go to the local CofE with Dad sometimes. I have a younger sister, but much of my extended family moved north years ago. Oh, I am so sorry, talking about myself. Come on – what about you?"

Whilst Ronnie was rambling Thistle had been mentally preparing for this moment. She paused before replying whilst completing an appraisal: a good-looking, well-dressed specimen, professional, older and richer than the boys she knew. No hint of patchouli-infused 'weed'; Ronnie's scent was straight from a bottle of Brut. In a flash she decided to be economical with the truth but refrain from brazen lies.

❧

Ronnie had always felt blessed. His parents were orthodox but also reasonable and understanding. His father respected his mother, and her mothering was the type that didn't cling or judge. His father encouraged him in business, allowing him to make mistakes but ensuring that he learned from them. The only disquiet in his parents' lives was that Ronnie was still unmarried aged twenty-seven whereas his sister had wed aged twenty. Perhaps this was why Ronnie himself, despite his appearance and wealth, had become concerned with his inability to locate a partner for life. His parents' relationship was unusual in its mixture of parity and passion. Demonstrations of affection were commonplace. Their love was a light that burned brightly. Ronnie was beset by a lurking fear that he could never hold a candle to compare.

"You'll love her… she's adorable," he said to his parents about Thistle, in the same way he had described Polly, the puppy he had brought home five years beforehand when he still resided with them. By Christmas 1974 Thistle had been welcomed into the family. It wasn't difficult to please Ronnie in a multitude of ways with the exception of sex. She knew that to secure his love she must go 'all the way'. This was the price to pay for surety of emotional tenure. It was like flipping a coin; sometimes it fell 'heads up' and the experience was relatively tolerable if she displaced herself from the reality of it. The other side of the coin held a disturbing and surreal visualisation which escaped her consciousness as fast as it had arrived.

Thistle spent most of her spare time at Ronnie's 1960s suburban end-of-terrace house erected in the middle of older properties on a cleared World War Two bomb site. "You might as well move in," he said, repeatedly.

"But – your parents… they would not approve."

"I know how to get around them." Ronnie was smiling. On Christmas Eve he presented Thistle with an engagement ring. White gold containing a sapphire to match her eyes. His parents were overjoyed. Thistle was overcome. If only she could genuinely love Ronnie in the way she was pretending to. January 1975 saw her pack up her few belongings and, with no regret, say farewell to the bed-sit. Ronnie's house was on the eastern side of the city, near to the estuary. It was also a dreary bus ride followed by a long walk to the gas board offices, so he bought her a moped. Her clerical assistant duties had been upgraded but Thistle struggled with office confinement. Escape from this presented itself when Ronnie began talking about their future wedding.

"Once you are my wife there will be no need for you to work… well, except if you want to… maybe occasionally helping me? You don't like it at the gas board, do you? I mean – unless you want to continue."

Of course, she didn't. *Bring this wedding on*, she thought.

"Ronnie, let's not wait too long."

"Weddings take planning, so it won't be before your eighteenth birthday." He took her hand, giving it a squeeze. In the weeks that followed Thistle began to agonise over the wedding. She was uneasy about Ronnie's family and friends witnessing her fabricate public vows. Her eighteenth birthday was celebrated by a meal out with Ronnie, his parents, sister and brother-in-law. That was enough focus on counterfeit enactments by the cute girl with ice-blonde hair and cool blue eyes. She had a dream that it was her wedding day and as she stood in glory at the front of the altar, a hand dropped down from the nave and ripped the white dress of innocence from her shoulders to expose a membrane of slippery scales, a snake.

Ronnie and Thistle eloped in May 1975. His parents, at first reeling with shock and disappointment, forgave them and, in line with their benign approach to life, accepted the couple's action. "At least this means they can start a family," chirruped his mother, in eagerness. Thistle's continual presence in Ronnie's house enabled the return of Polly, who had been cared for by Ronnie's mother since he acquired his own home. Thistle enjoyed breathing in sea air as she walked Polly along the tidal estuary's shingle beach. She became fascinated by the towering, regal cruise liners which regularly docked at the port. "Sail away," she whispered, "with me." Thistle was always somewhere else in her imagination but for now she focussed on life's fulfilling factors. The necessity to work having disappeared provided her with plenty of time to fashion the home after the essence of Thistle, beginning with the garden. She remembered all that Eric and Vida had taught her, but amongst a palette of border bedding plants she would always allow a wild purple bloom protected by barbed spikes to survive. Horticultural improvements were followed by the interior: beige and bland, every room needed coats of perkily shaded emulsion and sharp, snowy gloss. Thistle discovered a natural dexterity in the use of sandpaper and paintbrush. Relaxation was available at any time; for her eighteenth birthday Ronnie had purchased a light oak-veneered piano. This completed the Thistle-designed tapestry of domestic blissfulness. Ronnie worked long hours. Thistle remained in contact with Ruth; she would scooter over to see her from time to time. Ruth now lived with Jed on the bottom floor of a converted house, creating glass mosaics and weaving ethnic-style rugs and throws. Thistle had nothing in common with her, but the familiarity was reassuring and evidenced that Thistle had 'history'.

Sundays would be spent at Ronnie's parents' house. His sister, brother-in-law and their small child were always in attendance. Thistle had no connection with any of them either and found conversation contrived and awkward. Ronnie's mother presented a miscellany of dishes from the Punjab. Thistle watched the preparation: specific amounts of a variety of spices would be patiently ground whilst finely chopped onions, sautéing in oil or ghee, would eventually be united with smashed cloves of garlic and grated wedges of ginger. The spice mixture complete, it was either dry-fried or mixed into a paste with a drop of liquid, sometimes coconut oil. Meat, fish or lentils provided protein, and side dishes of vegetables received their own unique blend of flavours. Stock, water or coconut milk completed the sauce, stew or gravy. Local supermarkets did not sell all the components, or most of the necessary spices; Ronnie's mother had to travel to the city's Indian quarter for those. This community had ensured that the ingredients of its historical and cultural gastronomy would always be plentiful upon the shelves of its many corner stores. Thistle attempted to produce imitations for Ronnie; this required her to accompany his mother to the Indian sector. Thistle was nervous of walking its streets alone, not because of the ethnic population but because the area overlapped with an infamous 'red-light' district. Ronnie was highly appreciative of her efforts. In fact, he was incredibly satisfied with the world he had created.

Seasons sauntered by. During the fiercely hot summer of 1976 the house became unbearably oppressive. "We need somewhere bigger... airier," said Ronnie. By 1977 they lived in a detached house built of flax-coloured bricks, on the boundary of a quaint village a few miles east along the estuary. It was also a yachting destination. Thistle's name was not entered on the deeds or the mortgage; she made no financial contributions, therefore Ronnie's Dad had advised him in this matter. She was unconcerned, being only too ecstatic at a change of scene and the novelty of refurbishing and revitalising a rather neglected house and garden. Ronnie became known in the local community as an ambitious, assiduous and affable businessman. Offers of sailing expeditions came through a social network he slipped into via the village's pub clientele. Ronnie relished this new hobby and bought a share in a medium-sized sailing craft. Thistle's reaction was unsurprising: "I'm sorry, Ronnie, but I really don't have sea legs so would rather stay at home." Had he bought a slice of a cruise liner she may have been more enthusiastic. Ronnie's sailing fraternity asked little about Thistle. Her elfish beauty carried with it an aura of mystique; it easily outshone the medallion hung around his neck or the burnished rings wrapped around his fingers. She completed Ronnie's picture-book of achievements. No-one in the village community questioned her reclusiveness; it was never wise to make assumptions or cast aspersions. Whilst out exercising Polly she would comment on the weather with a couple of elderly villagers, then retreat to her own anchorage. Thistle's inner world bobbed, tossed and sometimes sailed along its own estuary – being the inlet to the pianist's interpretation of song. The consequence of Ronnie's commitment to both business and sailing was of less and less time that he spent at home. Sometimes curries would be left uneaten. Often sex was a brief encounter and not of the quintessential romantic kind.

"No pregnancy… over four years on," bemoaned Ronnie's mother to his father. "Tina is on her second. There must be a problem – perhaps Thistle is infertile. What then? We need heirs to the businesses, but it isn't just that… Ronnie is such a dear. He would make a wonderful dad. He would love to take his children out sailing… What are we to do?"

Her husband's face crinkled in slight amusement. "*Mere pyare*, there is nothing we can 'do'. But I will open up a conversation about it with him."

Ronnie himself was pondering on how to touch upon the same subject with Thistle, but it seemed that they hardly spoke to one another anymore. He made the decision to buy Thistle an erotic nightie; her regular sleep attire was pyjamas. *What size?* He had not noticed whether she had gained or lost weight and thought it wise to check. She was walking Polly when he discreetly investigated her lingerie drawer. His fingers rested on a metallic papered surface, and he retrieved the object. It was a tiny, rectangular packet with twenty-one miniscule openings. His blood began to boil like the bubbling magma of a volcano. As Thistle entered the hallway the packet landed at her feet; propelled with the force of a missile, it narrowly missed her chin. Polly ran into the kitchen. "*Out!*" Ronnie raged like the proverbial bull confronted with a red rag. "*Go on, go*, and take your pills to prevent pregnancy with you!" His face had become bulbous with ferocity. Thistle's feet felt grounded to the spot. Something inside recoiled into a tight knot of restraint.

"I wasn't ready." She tried to enthuse her words with sincerity.

"*Are you ready now?*"

Thistle couldn't lie – not on this occasion.

Ronnie regained some self-control. "I am taking Polly over to Mum and Dad's. I will stay there until the end of the week. On my return I don't want to find you or your paltry possessions still here, and by the way, the piano belongs to *me*." Ronnie could not diffuse the tide of emotion, a tornado that whirled within him. He had furnished Thistle with everything that should have guaranteed her loyalty. At thirty-two years old a sinkhole had appeared in his impeccable, personal construct of the status quo. This was not the marriage of his parents. He had been deceived. Thistle was metaphorically at the bottom of a cliff with no way to climb back up. She knew this.

"Ruth." The telephone lead lay flaccid in her hand. "It's me, Thistle. I need a place to stay – know of anywhere? Yes – now, well, in the next couple of days. *Please*, Ruth, I'm homeless…" Ruth promised to contact everyone she knew.

Thistle had no knowledge of her rights. She knew that she would miss the house and Polly, especially the latter, but she would not miss Ronnie at all. It was a fact that she had never loved him and therefore it was only deserving that she bow out of his life graciously. Ronnie's father advised that Ronnie give Thistle a financial allowance to cover her rent and living expenses until she found employment. Ronnie's mother convinced him that the breakup was karma. After a two-year separation divorce would sever the tie, forever. Ruth had a friend of a friend with a bed-sit to rent at Bistead, just a mile from where Thistle had first lived with Ronnie but not close to the estuary. It was a ground-floor room at the front of a seared-vermillion brick house of late Victorian architecture. Larger than her first bed-sit, through discoloured net curtains which hung in the sash window she could see four feet of scrubby grass, fronted by a low brick wall. On the other side was a tarmac road and a mixture of housing styles. The interior walls were plain and painted powder blue, which amplified the frostiness that the room seemed sprinkled with. Mid-October 1979 and the weather was unusually mild, but these soulless four walls emanated only indifference and detachment, in contrast to Steve, who owned the building and lived on the top floor. He was an imperious, stocky man who falsely believed that women could not resist his charm. His breath smelled of over-boiled cabbage as he leaned closely in to Thistle, explaining that the rent could be lowered in return for 'small favours'. She felt bilious and resolved to thwart all and every advance. The bathroom was shared with another man who was disinterested in forging any type of relationship. It took a number of moped journeys to collect and deposit Thistle's clothes and personal effects. As she left her home, Ronnie's house for the final time, she took a last look at the piano. Upon it a silver-framed photo of Polly sat on a lace surface protector. Thistle's eyes began to sting. Holding back her tears, she drew in the deepest breath; it seemed to sink to her toes from where it escaped into the gilded stillness of an autumn eventide.

Ronnie's rehearsed explanation to his friends was that Thistle had apparently suffered a 'breakdown', resulting in her falling into the arms of a woman, a feminist.

"Always thought her strange," said one; the yachting clique all nodded in agreement.

# 3

# Same City:
# January 1980

Hᴵʟᴀʀʏ's ꜰɪɴɢᴇʀᴛɪᴘs ʀᴀᴘᴘᴇᴅ the dining table in annoyance. *She's late… not a good start.* Moments later the doorbell exploded with sound, and as Hilary opened the door Fliss almost fell upon her.

"So sorry I am late." She began longwinded explanations, only to be interrupted by Hilary: "Never mind, you are here now and… wait a moment, I recognise you."

Absorbing this comment, Fliss took a long look at Hilary as they entered a lounge diner. There was something familiar about this young woman of roughly Fliss's age. She had pale skin, shoulder-length, moth-shade hair and her oval face was dominated by a large pair of tortoiseshell, plastic-rimmed spectacles. Clothed in dowdy, faded green corduroy trousers with a buff-coloured wool sweater hanging heavily from her shoulders, Hilary was in complete contrast to the attractive, black-haired, chic female dressed in designer denim who stood in front of her. "Please take a seat—"

"Secondary school!" exclaimed Fliss. "I remember now. We were in the same year, but you were in the top sets. I was two sets down in most subjects."

"Of course." Hilary studied this face from the past; above fine, high cheekbones sat honey-brown eyes which glinted with the sharpness of a bird of prey.

"You're Felice Watson, known to all as 'Fliss.'"

"Hilary... sorry, I cannot remember your surname. What a coincidence."

"Ummm," grunted Hilary, unsure of whether this was a good omen or not.

"So Fliss – you are looking for a room to rent, lodgings?"

"Yes, indeed," Fliss replied, and, using ten words for every single word where just one would have sufficed, explained her situation. She had been living in Normandy, France, for over five years, caring for her French great-aunt Amelie and working in the produce shop on a farm owned by Amelie's brother, Fliss's great-uncle, and his son. The great-aunt died last October and Fliss decided to return home in November. (She omitted a particular reason for this decision.) However, now her parents were moving house. Her elder brother Philip and his wife were expecting a baby, and Fliss's mum wanted to live closer to them. Her dad could live anywhere as his position in the local authority was county-wide. Fliss's parents had offered on a property, had a buyer for theirs and the sale was going through. Their move out to the forest, near Philip, would mean a tiresome drive into the city centre for Fliss, where she had gained employment in a department store, Williams and Brown. She did not admit that in addition, living back home with parents was cramping her style, especially where men were concerned. "So – that's it, in a nutshell," she finished.

*More a coconut shell*, thought Hilary.

"Well," said Hilary, "as you can see, this is not a house, but as maisonettes go it is large enough for two people to co-exist."

"When we spoke on the phone, you said that you own this place."

It was Hilary's turn for explanations. Her curt delivery took only a few minutes.

"Godmother died... had no kids and left me enough for a deposit on a property; seemed like a wise investment. As a senior librarian I am paid quite well, but bills and maintenance necessitates a top-up." Hilary did not disclose her own reasons for escaping parental control.

"Do you work in the city library, at the back of the civic centre?"

"Yes. It's only a twenty-five-minute bus ride."

"If I move in I could give you a lift – if our hours are the same."

"You mentioned that you have a car."

"A Renault Twelve TL. I notice you have a parking space outside and a driveway. Ideal."

Hilary considered this. Her hours would probably not always match Fliss's, but even an occasional lift would save her from the daily sick-making ride in a cigarette smoke-filled bus. Then she noticed the tip of a packet of cigarettes protruding from Fliss's bag.

"You smoke?"

Fliss took out a light blue, soft-shelled carton. "Gauloises. They're French. Would you like one?"

"I don't smoke. Waste of money."

"Obviously I wouldn't smoke indoors if it annoyed you."

"The covered porch would be a useful place in winter. And I guess if the weather is too bad an occasional one would do no harm. Let me show you around. You can see whether you like it."

Fliss made a more detailed survey of the lounge diner, which, similar to Hilary's face, was also dominated by a large item – a piano.

"Do you play, Hilary?"

"Badly, I'm afraid."

The spare bedroom was of good size with a pine double wardrobe. This was important, as Fliss had an abundance of clothes. Her eyes lit up. "I work on the ladies' fashion floor." Tour complete, they went outside. "You have a garden – how fabulous." Fliss knew nothing about gardening, but summer sunbathing was a crucial constituent of her existence.

"It's just lawn and some old shrubs, really, but I have plans to create flowerbeds like the ones in the smaller patch of garden at the front – which also belongs to me. Do you notice those broken pieces of an old bath? I intend on using them in a rockery."

"What are the people on the upper floor like?"

"A professional couple. Very quiet, and as they have external steps to their front door, I hardly ever see them. On the other side of my shed is a path which leads down to an area of grass which is their garden, but they hardly use it."

"Other neighbours?"

"A few working gentlemen, that's it." The word 'gentlemen' teased itself into Fliss's ears.

Fliss wanted to move in before Hilary had a chance to change her mind. Hilary realised that Fliss's sparkly personality reminded her of a childhood friend; plus she had found that living alone for three months was quite isolating. She wasn't going to change her mind. After Fliss had left, Hilary's memory took her on a journey to revisit herself as a thirteen-year-old schoolgirl, included was that treasured 'old friend' and what occurred after the friend had moved away. It was because of a photo of the young man Hilary had met on holiday, his blackness and the subsequent ridicule; that's what started it. Girls in groups can become ruthless and intimidating when they espy vulnerable prey. If only she had not taken the photo into school, but even if she hadn't done so, the bullying was already brewing. Hilary was as 'different' as he had been 'black'. Elderly religious parents enforced acquiescence to social norms at complete odds with the culture of 1960s England. Old-fashioned hand-me-down clothes, National Health specs and a pudding-bowl haircut ensured that Hilary stood out from the crowd in a most unattractive way. Hilary had held her own as best as she could, concentrating on her studies and clawing a path through the bindweed of peer persecution and parental oppression. Fliss, being in lower attainment classes except for French language, was never one of her tormentors. The transition to sixth form college relieved Hilary's situation; at sixteen years of age the bullies all decided to go straight into employment (as had Fliss); it was abundant in this cargo and passenger port city, famous for naval ship-building and aircraft construction. Hilary made a close friend in Gaye and for two years the sixth form college girls enjoyed sparring with boys, mooching around street corners and experimenting with alcohol. All of which was unnoticed by Hilary's parents, whose health concerns and pious 'good works' continued to be their focus of attention. Hilary had never been regarded central to their lives. When younger she found their attitudes and behaviour, their implicit negligence hurtful. By sixteen years of age, it was welcomed. In 1973, after achieving success in her 'A' Level examinations, Hilary found employment as a junior librarian not far from home. Gaye exceeded everyone's expectations with her results. Unfortunately the outcome was her leaving to study medicine at a northern university. "We'll stay in touch," she reassured Hilary. University campus life commanded differently. Letters became fewer and friendship ebbed away like retreating waves as they suck at the water's edge.

Fliss moved in on the first Saturday that both young women were not on a rota to work. Her mum Marguerite, a well-dressed woman in her early fifties with Gallic bone structure and palomino-tinted hair, inspected the 'new' home on the pretext of assisting Fliss carry endless bags of clothing.

"Hello, Hilary," Marguerite introduced herself. "I don't expect you remember me, but I can recall you, and your parents. I used to chat to your mother at school parents' evenings and other functions. I particularly remember that she and your father spent a lot of time at Christmas organising toys for deprived children in the area, and I understand that they invited disabled kids home all year round. They were always involved in charitable work, despite their medical conditions. So very Christian. They were entirely committed to the Methodist church. Devout people. Stalwarts of the community."

Hilary suppressed a grimace. Marguerite did not notice; she was relieved to discover that Fliss would be living with the plain, sensible daughter of respectable people.

By late morning Fliss was ensconced and Marguerite had departed. Apart from clothes and cosmetics, Fliss had relatively little clutter. A cafetière, which she had dragged back from France with her, was placed onto the kitchen counter along with a bottle of red wine.

"Has to be real coffee…"

"I drink tea," said Hilary, putting the kettle on and eyeing the red wine.

"Wine – for us to celebrate my first night here!" Fliss curled up her lips into an expression – a smirk, for which she was famous. "Oh, sorry, Hilary – do you drink alcohol? Hearing about your folks being Methodists."

Hilary opened a cupboard door to reveal cans of lager and a bottle of Martini.

"But I'm not." For the first time Hilary grinned, displaying a perfectly aligned set of white teeth.

*Thank goodness*, thought Fliss. "What about food? Obviously I'm keen on French cookery."

"I can cook, but by the time I get home from work I can't be bothered, so it's often sausages or fish fingers with baked beans. But sometimes I make spaghetti Bolognese."

Fliss raised her eyebrows. "I like Italian food, but... look, before I went to France I had a flat share with a friend, and we took turns depending on which of us had the most time. How does that sound?"

Hilary agreed that this would make sense.

"So," continued Fliss, "I need to get some ingredients. Is there a supermarket nearby?"

"A Co-op, but the Sainsbury's up at Bistead has a larger range."

"After lunch we can drive up there and stock up."

Just before they left Fliss rushed to her car, pulled out the ashtray, emptied it into the dustbin and sprayed a little cologne to mask the acrid odour.

Fliss's fragrant Coq au Vin with warm baguette was much revered by Hilary and the wine loosened the tongues of these new friends. Hilary asked where the 'French connection' came from.

"Grandmamma, Mum's French mum, met an Englishman at the end of World War One, they married and she came to live in England. I am named after her but couldn't pronounce Felice. As a very young child I said 'Fliss', which I think suits me better!"

"Did your great-aunt have dementia?"

"Oh no. She was always weird. As a girl Great-Aunt Amelie was jilted at the altar and then had a stillborn baby. It must have affected her dreadfully because eventually she would only speak with 'spirits'. I thought they were fairies.

I know all of this because my poppa – that's what we called Grandpa – died when I was about five years old, so my grandmamma decided to return to France and care for her sister Amelie, who had become a strain on the French family. That's when we began visiting every year and I got to know the Normandy relations. In 1974 Grandmamma died so I offered to be Amelie's carer and also to work in the family farm shop for just a few francs spending money."

"But why?"

"Life was boring here; nineteen years old with an uninspiring boyfriend and trapped in office work… tedious to distraction! I discovered my flair for sales in the farm shop but now I much prefer the world of fashion."

"And…?" Trying to sound insightful, Hilary was attempting to focus her steel-grey eyes through a wonky blur of intoxication.

"You aren't daft, are you, Hilary! I sort of became girlfriend to two men and I couldn't decide between them…"

Fliss gulped down another glass of wine. Her honey-brown eyes, framed with thick, luscious lashes, peered at the empty bottle as if searching for a long-lost friend.

"How about a Martini then?"

Hilary was a little less forthcoming about how she had spent the adult portion of her twenty-four years. Fliss remembered her as a quiet schoolgirl and had assumed that her mother, appearing so old, was her grandmother. A few words conveyed the suffocation of Hilary's family home and the control exerted by strict adhesion to stringent religious and moral codes: "God was always watching me.

Other people were always less fortunate, so it was *always* better to give than to receive. It was also important, in fact required, to understand the scriptures and follow the Ten Commandments. Then there were sins of the flesh – crikey: never mention sex, it did not exist!"

*No wonder she isn't Methodist*, thought Fliss.

"Did you have to be a goody two-shoes all of the time?"

"Actually, there were many instances when I was far from it, but they were either so busy being goody two-shoes themselves or so poorly that they didn't notice me much, except when Mum felt like having verbal diarrhoea or gave me a list of jobs to do."

"I remember her. Thought she was like—"

"Machiavelli?" Hilary interrupted. "She has always been charming to everyone except her own family. Look at how she deviously conned your mother with her depiction of piety!"

Fliss had never heard of Machiavelli. "I was going to say… grandma in the Giles cartoons!"

Hilary smiled. "Yes – cranky and demanding. At times even Dad hides away from her. He is typical of his generation – utterly archaic, yet he lets her rule the roost."

"Brothers… sisters?" enquired Fliss, seeking strands of cheerfulness.

"Much older brother and sister. They escaped as soon as they could. Both live in Scotland – as far from Mother as possible."

"Have you not thought about joining them?"

Hilary's face froze in horror. "How could I do that? My parents are elderly now… the guilt should anything happen. I would never forgive myself."

Fliss realised that she had touched a nerve; its receptor triggered culpability.

Hilary anxiously diverted the conversation. "Your mum seems nice. I vaguely remember her from school events, but not your dad."

"God no – you wouldn't have seen him." Fliss's words were beginning to slur.

"He only had time for my brothers. Mum has always been a soft touch, but Dad is a fossil from the Ice Age. In fact, I don't think I can be their offspring. I must have been adopted. They are so... so conventional and boring." Fliss over-exaggerated a yawn, crossed her eyes, stretched out her arms and almost fell off the sofa. Hilary laughed; her lodger displayed a wacky sense of fun, despite the tendency to describe many aspects of life as 'boring'.

Sunday morning brought chinks of sunlight, puffy white clouds and keenly felt hangovers. Fliss persuaded Hilary to sample 'real coffee'. Neither could face food. Hilary outlined that her usual weekend routine involved visiting her parents for Sunday lunch but because of their morning church attendance that wasn't until two o'clock. The forty-minute walk there would do her good. Fliss had no intention of returning home where she would have been enmeshed in helping Marguerite fill packing boxes. A lingering soak in the bath followed by a horizontal view of the television were on her agenda. In coming weeks the habits and customs of Hilary and Fliss blended together like the velvety fruit sorbets which Fliss often whipped up. During the week and on occasional Saturdays, Hilary valued some lifts to and from work. In the evenings she continued with her temperate pastimes of reading, watching television and occasionally tinkling the ivories. Fliss did not read much, except *Cosmopolitan* magazine. She too enjoyed television but gradually Fliss became 'head chef', spending increasing amounts of time in the kitchen emulating her current culinary hero, Michel Guerard. She had brought his books back from France along with the cafetière and a couple of Le Creuset cooking pots. Friday and Saturday evenings saw Fliss in her favoured habitat, nightclubs, where she met up with the girls from work.

"It's such fun, Hilary. Why don't you come?"

Hilary was not convinced. Her weekend outings involved meeting a friend, Sandra, for tea and cake or cinema trips.

"Sandra and I began our library careers in Bistead when we were both eighteen. She married a man in the Navy who is at sea a lot of the time, so we are company for each other." Hilary could make relationships on a one-to-one basis but still struggled with female groups.

"I was bullied at school," she admitted to Fliss one day.

"I know," responded Fliss with carefully understated compassion. But she was not one to be easily deterred. Concerned that there had been no mention of romance in Hilary's history, Fliss began to consider manoeuvres to overcome Hilary's resistance and introduce her to the world of flirtation.

Being flirtatious – that is what had evolved from Fliss's childhood wilfulness. The flashing of her eyes, once upon a time adopted to convey insolence and insurgence, had mutated; now it engendered sensual mystery and sexual intrigue. Men could be ensnared, like stricken flies decomposing in a spider's web. Fliss sniggered at her own analogy. The reality of her ability to enthral persistently brought about tricky situations, as it had in France. Alain had appeared at the farm in August 1977 searching for casual work apple-picking. Having finished university, he was seeking a way to avoid returning to his family's heritable enterprise, a Chateau Vineyard in the Loire Valley. His lascivious eyes carbon-copied Fliss's and his beguile was a match for her own. To embark upon a passionate affair was inevitable. Alain stayed on through that following winter odd-jobbing on the farm. Fliss's Great-Uncle Claude's son Didier, who now managed the Normandy cheese and cider business, was glad of another strong farmhand to add to his team; Didier had been bestowed with daughters. Was Fliss's eventual boredom with Alain part of her personality? She often contemplated as to why, when the fervour of lust had cooled, her relationships with men always dwindled into monotony. Then, in early spring 1979, Alain was called home; his grandpapa was dying. "*Au revoir a ma cherie Fliss, tu me manqueras tellement.*"

"English, Alain! Speak to me in English – you know that you master it very well. I will miss you too, darling. *Soyez bon... se comporter!*"

"And be good yourself, my flirty Fliss!" Alain hugged her with candid craving. Asking either young person to 'be good' was as futile as requesting apples not to fall from burdened trees. Jerome was employed to replace Alain. A local lad and four years younger than her, Jerome had been dreaming about Fliss since her arrival in 1974. Initially he was always keen to pop to the farm shop for his mama, but then he developed acne so kept away. Facial lesions having disappeared, he was now an unobtrusive, lean and sallow-skinned young man, but his arms displayed muscles which secured him the work and told a story of cloistered potency. Fliss was captivated. Jerome was putting tools away when Fliss leaned nonchalantly against the shed door; she had perfected this stance over the years. Her lips curled into that familiar smirk; her eyes danced like cherubs at a fountain. Tantalised beyond self-constraint, Jerome's bodily thermostat ascended with alacrity. Fliss kicked the door shut with her foot as two collared doves fluttered out through a hole in the roof, their wings beating similarly to the pulsating hearts of two trembling humans lurking in the semi-darkness beneath them.

Alain's papa persuaded him to stay on for a while, trying to entice his eldest child and only son to take an interest in the vineyard. Alain's degree had been in business management – he was supposed to have returned to Chateau Veronique after graduating. By August Alain was missing Fliss too much. He had been kept entertained by a country girl with coquettish manners and a partiality for l'affaire du Coeur, but she could not surpass the polish and panache of Fliss; her wit and intuition had captured more than just his loins. Didier was glad of all the help he could get; business was thriving and by then he had learned of Alain's commercial acumen. Fliss panicked but there was nothing she could do. She had to reveal her affair with Jerome. Alain could hardly criticise Fliss and admitted his own infidelity, but she was not ready to disengage from Jerome's attention. The unsatisfactory solution was the establishment of a 'ménage de trois'. Neither man could cut the reins that bound him to Fliss.

"You must decide, *ma chere Felice*," implored Didier. "It is not the face of the business to have such a household. It does not make for successful teamwork between Alain and Jerome... and most importantly, you are setting a very bad example to my daughters!"

For a usually decisive young woman, Fliss was ambivalent. Then in October 1979 Great-Aunt Amelie peacefully passed away. Fliss had a strange feeling that something significant was going to happen weeks before it occurred; somehow she knew it would solve her problem. "Thank you, dear Amelie," she whispered in her dead great-aunt's ear, "Did your spirit friends call upon you to join them or did you recognise my predicament? *Merci chere Amelie, tu resteras dans mon Coeur.*"

Fliss declined Didier's offer to increase the hours she worked for him.

"Didier, it is time for me to leave..." She winked. He understood. By November Fliss was lying alone in her childhood bed, surrounded by the trappings of a city upbringing, and reunited with her diligent, undemonstrative English father and warm-hearted, long-suffering half-French mother.

❧

"Hilary, have you ever thought about having your hair permed?"

Hilary looked down her nose at Fliss. It was a learned librarian expression useful as mental punishment for borrowers returning overdue books. "No, certainly not. Your hair isn't permed."

Fliss heaved her chest. "That's because it is cut in a French bob style, which doesn't look right permed! It was just an idea… oh yes, could you do me a favour? I need to practise dressing mannequins to full sales effect. Could I practise on you? Using my clothes, of course."

"*Your* clothes?"

"Well, underneath the baggy tents you wear I think you are about my size."

"I have a thick waist."

"Please, Hilary – my manager says I should be extending my skillset."

Hilary's dour expression relaxed into a broad smile. "Oh, Fliss, you are certainly extending your acting skills, do you think I was born yesterday?!"

"It will be fun… how about some wine and a few martinis?"

It was the evening of Thursday 3rd of April. The next day was Good Friday so neither of them had to work. Hangovers always had a time and place.

And it was fun. Fliss had purchased a full-length, floor-standing mirror. With guile she dressed Hilary in a range of padded-shouldered garments, drawn in not too tightly at the waist and swanky with suggestive sophistication.

"Hilary – you're a bobby-dazzler." Despite the wine Hilary's eyes could focus and she gaped at her own reflection. No words came, just alcohol-induced tears.

"I'll do your makeup if you like—"

"No – not like this," wailed Hilary.

"I'm sorry… I did not mean to upset you."

"I know. It's… it's just… maybe I'm better off hiding away under 'tents.'"

"No, Hilary. You have the right to broadcast all your assets, physical as well as mental. And you also have a right to…"

"To love?" Hilary composed herself. "I'm not sure what that is."

For the first time since being five years old Fliss remained silent. Hilary had important things to divulge. Give a person space and they will fill it.

"I think I fell in love aged thirteen, on holiday. He was older than me and studying to be a minister, so he was perfectly behaved. I was supposed to write to him but when I took his photo to school the girls saw what I hadn't noticed. Why would I? I was brought up to know adults and children of different ethnicities; sometimes they also had disabilities. I saw a kind, understanding and wonderfully handsome young man. My classmates saw only blackness… the colour of his skin. I don't know why but I threw his address away. So you see, no matter how infuriating my parents are, they are not dishonourable – as I am."

Fliss topped up Hilary's wine glass. "But surely you were just recoiling from peer pressure – are you saying you haven't looked at anyone since?"

Hilary looked straight into Fliss's eyes, which registered genuine concern. She continued, "It must have been near Christmas 1974. I was still working at Bistead Library and had made friends with Sandra. A guy, again a bit older than me, started chatting when he came in to change books. He asked me out for a drink and was good company. I told my mother I was seeing Sandra. Then he suggested he cook me a meal; he had his own flat. Heck, I was so naïve. I'm sure you can guess what took place."

"He forced himself upon you?"

"It was horrible. I was drunk and he was rough. I think I was just a conquest, a notch on his bedpost, because he never borrowed any more books after that."

Hilary had no tears now, just an expression of resignation. "And before you ask – I am obviously a very slow learner because a similar thing happened during the hot summer of 1976. I saw that moron quite a few times. He borrowed money from me, but I didn't mind; he made me feel normal… at last I had a boyfriend, or so I thought. I turned up at his place unexpected one day to find him romping under the sheets with his brother's girlfriend. I never got my money back… can remember the exact figure. It was one hundred pounds. Fliss, men notice me approaching with the same clarity as they view a vividly illuminated ocean liner chugging up the estuary."

"No-one else…?"

"Only Charles, the son of friends of my parents. He could make dishwater appear lively. Charles would recite complete passages from the Bible without a hint of comprehension or emotion, and when he sang hymns it was also like those cruise liners, well – their fog horns! Mum kept inviting him around for tea and leaving us on our own. It was like living in Victorian times. His attempts to kiss me resembled the slobber of a doting dog and that's what he would have become, if I had allowed him. That is not 'love', is it? Anyway, a position came up at the city library where there would be more opportunities for promotion. It entailed longer hours at work and travelling by bus – there was no time for 'tea.'"

Hilary had composed herself and managed a wispy smile.

"Hilary, I promise I will never, ever try to persuade you to go off with any man – although I think the right one has not yet come along, and I am sure he will. But... it is my twenty-fifth birthday in three weeks, and I would love for you to come out with me and the girls from work. You can wear whatever you like the best from this lot. Will you at least think about it?"

Hilary did not want to go clubbing but neither did she wish to disappoint Fliss, who was becoming a trusted friend. On Friday 25th April she and Fliss managed to leave their workplaces a little earlier than usual in preparation for the grand night out. That morning Hilary presented Fliss with a well-chosen gift; a pop-art poster of Picasso's *Le Moulin De La Galette*, portraying Parisian café culture of 1900. Fliss was pleasantly taken aback and appreciated the effort Hilary must have made trekking around department stores to find such a gem. Hilary permitted Fliss to repeat the mannequin parade, emerging in a knee-length, A-line black party dress featuring a scalloped neckline and elbow-length sleeves. The viscose cloth shimmered with random red and gold sequins. It was one of Fliss's more restrained outfits. Hilary's feet had to squeeze into a pair of Fliss's matching red and gold sling-backs. Fliss was careful not to daub Hilary's face with an excess of colour; the overall result was stylish and pleasing on the eye. Fliss herself was striking in a three quarter-length ink-black skirt which dashingly flaunted a long slit up one side, coupled with a tightly fitted, burgundy silk blouse. High-heeled black ankle-strap shoes enabled Fliss to have the height she regretted not possessing. Skilful with cosmetics, her portrayal was of a classy femme fatale.

The evening began at Mario's Ristorante, a trendy, upbeat Italian restaurant central to the city's nightlife zone. Intending on drinking even more than normal, Fliss had suggested that they travel there by bus and return by taxi. *That's a relief*, thought Hilary, who was unnerved by how Fliss regularly handled her Renault after downing many brandy and lemonades – Fliss's usual club-scene tipple. Five young dazzling damsels, colleagues from Williams and Brown, joined them at the table. Pizzas were washed down with carafes of Valpolicella. The atmosphere was electrified by the energy of exuberant diners and the raucous playing of traditional troubadour music. Hilary felt exhausted by the time they left for Bertie's, a fashionable club with high-tech lighting and a dancefloor divided into two levels by palatial synthetic pillars. The other girls seemed companionable enough, but the wine was more interesting than the banality of their conversation. To arrive at Bertie's was a tottering stroll for seven sets of pins balancing on stiletto heels. A doorman ushered them in; his mouth wore a contorted leer of recognition. Coats were left with an usherette, who slovenly hung them on distorted metal hangers. Double doors opened into a world beyond Hilary's understanding. A richly lyrical voice was warbling like a song thrush on a summer morning:

*"Night world voyaging, the bar and dancefloor call me, can anyone see through me? A connoisseur of carousels – a ghost among the crowd. Night world voyaging..."*

Hilary did not recognise the vocals of a hit single that was accurately interpreting many people's experience of clubbing. She gazed around at phantom figures propped against bars, columns and what appeared to be tethering posts. Intense light would suddenly shoot across the semi-darkness in rhythm with the bassline beat of catchy, dance-friendly disco sounds. Fliss twisted her torso in time with the other girls. *The Dionysus-inspired ecstatic frenzy of Maenads*, observed Hilary. She did not realise that her own unmoving body was under the constant watchfulness of two people: Fliss, who was inwardly listening to an instinct to protect Hilary; and a slim, mousy-haired man sporting a stone-grey shirt, charcoal slacks and harmonising bomber jacket.

Fliss and dancing partners joined Hilary at a small table near one of the bars. Fliss, with her usual feline sway, wandered over to collect drinks. Pairs of tom-cat eyes followed her every move. Before long four young men were vying for her attention, volunteering to carry the drinks tray, offering her cigarettes. The tray arrived bearing six glasses; Fliss, with her brandy and lemonade, remained at the bar. The smell of Gauloises filtered across to irritate

Hilary's nostrils. The Williams and Brown girls sprung into feverish discussion. Hilary vacated herself in order to track down the ladies' toilet. Inside it she found a smoke-filled muddle. A girl sat on the floor howling whilst a brood of hens encircled her, uttering clucking sounds between the puffing of fags and slurping of cocktails. One cubicle was splattered with vomit, another littered with used Tampax. The washbasins were clogged with paper tissues and the bin overflowing with discarded contents from ladies' handbags. Hilary suddenly lost the urge to wee. Returning to the dancefloor, she peered through a mix of pin-spot and strobe lighting, searching for a familiar group of gaggling geese, Fliss's work colleagues.

"Would you like a drink?" The voice beside her was low and controlled.

Hilary hesitated. Was she about to be 'chatted up'? A murmur slipped out from her lips.

"You would like a red wine? So be it – won't be a moment."

Hilary would have walked away but for the lesson of politeness embedded in her as a child. *If he is getting me a drink it would be rude to disappear – and what if he spotted me across the room? What would I say?* It would have been bad-mannered not to remain.

A glass of wine was passed to her with the words, "So what has brought a refined young lady like you into this den of vice and iniquity?"

Hilary liked his use of words. *A reader*, she thought, and began to relax. "A friend's birthday..." Conversation remained at the shallow level expected of artificially arranged social situations. Quite soon it sounded as if the DJ had pumped up the volume as the words 'Disco delirium' jetted across the club.

"Shall we go outside?" suggested the man, who had revealed his name, but Hilary had not heard it above the din of Friday-night revellers. She welcomed the opportunity to escape both smog and the bellowing blare of speaker cabinets. The air was cool and refreshing, but Hilary began to perspire. *All the wine has gone to my head*, she thought as her body unsteadily inclined itself towards the man. He angled his arm around Hilary's waist and led her to a corner wall at the rear of Bertie's. Hilary noticed the moon. *Waxing gibbous… it will be full in four days*. The man was panting. She felt his tongue lick her neck as his hand lunged between her legs. Suddenly, without warning, the man cried out in pain as he abruptly withdrew his weight from Hilary's unbalanced form, falling backwards in the process. He grasped his own leg. Fliss pushed him away with the ease of a weightlifter. The expanding moon had acted as a spotlight upon the back of a slim, mousy-haired man wearing dark slacks and a bomber jacket.

Fliss's self-assured arm was swiftly draped around Hilary's shoulders, guiding her back towards Bertie's entrance vestibule. "Hilary, let's get our coats, find a taxi and go home."

"What did you do to him?"

"Brought my stiletto heel hard down onto his foot then kneed him in the thigh – the bastard deserved at least that!"

"I'm sorry, Fliss… and we can't go yet – it's your birthday." Hilary began to grizzle; Fliss offered her a tissue.

"We are going – end of. I am only twenty-five… I will have many more birthdays. Anyway, it seems I have four suitors and I am getting into rather a pickle about them."

"And your liver must be in a keg of pickle too," replied Hilary, squeezing out a smidgeon of a smile from her crestfallen face. Fliss pulled an impish grin. The two linked arms and made a safe journey home from the gals, ghouls and frequent fools of 'night world'.

# 4

# Thistle

OCTOBER 1979 MERGED with December without noticing
November. Thistle's day always began with her sat at a
counter which formed a part of the bed-sit's kitchenette.
Over a large mug of tea, she scoured newspaper-advertised
job vacancies. There was always an abundance of clerical
positions, but she was reluctant to re-enter an arena
apparently designed to house pointless activity. Later on
each morning she would wander around Bistead looking
at ads placed in shop windows. After a measly lunch and
weather permitting, her entertainment was to scooter off to
a free carpark from where she could walk along the estuary,
imagining a dog lead swinging from her hand. Thistle had
found her old television in the loft before leaving Ronnie's.
She paid a taxi to transport it to the bed-sit. Remarkably it
was still in working order. Ronnie had asked for proof of her

rent. He sent her a weekly cheque to cover it and provide the minimum required for food and sundries. From this income she had saved enough to buy a small artificial Christmas tree, a few baubles and tresses of silvery tinsel from a second-hand shop. Ruth had invited Thistle to spend Christmas day with herself and Jed. She was grateful for the offer but troubled by her lack of funds; she felt obliged to buy gifts and her allowance would not run to that. Then, one crisp mid-December morning she received a letter from Ronnie. It stated that he would not continue to finance her forever and he expected that she would have found employment by January. Thistle ripped the letter up. She did not venture outside that day. Panda was tittivated with spare tinsel.

At nine o'clock the following evening a knock came at the door. It was Steve (the landlord of bad breath). He clutched a bottle of whisky in one hand and a large bag of crisps in the other. "Thistle, it's nearly Christmas – the season of goodwill – so I have come to share my festive cheer with you, dear girl." Lips oozing spittle were stretched across his ruddy, pitted face. His smile was wider than that of any Cheshire cat, from rhyme or reality.

"Where's Kitten?" Kitten was Steve's sixteen-year-old, part-time girlfriend.

"Carol service." His mouth opened to reveal a gaping grotto; Thistle noticed the yellow of his teeth against the rosiness of his tongue.

"Okay – why not. Come in…"

It took quite an amount of whisky before Thistle slid her arm around his neck and pulled him towards her. "Rent reduction?" she whispered in his ear.

His reply was short: "Let's go upstairs – I have a double bed."

Giving her body for financial reward was easier than she had anticipated. She did not have to pretend to enjoy the occasion; indeed, Steve seemed unconcerned whether she did or didn't. She remembered how she would completely switch off from what eventually became rapid and loveless sex with Ronnie, by taking an almost astral excursion, which was far advanced to daily fantasising, closer to mental displacement. Unknown to Thistle, it was a form of self-hypnosis. She applied the same tactic. Thistle visualised a cruise ship leaving for an adventure with its passengers enthusiastically waving at an envious crowd cheering from the shoreline. The next moment she was on board amongst the passengers, looking towards the horizon with excitement and expectancy. A mighty groan concluded the proceedings. "I can keep the next two weeks' rent then?" Steve grunted in agreement, rolled onto his back and fell asleep. Thistle noticed a roll of ten-pound notes poking out from a wallet on his bedside table. She furtively filched one note, gathered up her clothes and headed for the shared bathroom. *A bonus payment for good servicing.* Thistle could always justify her actions. The long-term problem of employment was not solved, but the purchasing of gifts for Ruth and Jed had been.

Due to restricted Christmas banking hours Ronnie paid two weeks of allowance in one cheque which was immediately deposited into Thistle's TSB account. Steve never noticed the missing ten-pound note, with which Thistle bought more whisky and cans of cider. She felt flush with cash but was also keenly aware that January was less than a fortnight away. Most job vacancies were found in the Thursday edition of the local newspaper. On Thursday December 20th there was very little on offer except a small ad which caught Thistle's eye: 'Painter and decorator required for local firm. Good rates of pay. Call...' Despite bucketing rain Thistle hurried along to the nearest phone box and rang the number. After explaining her interest in the position, a man's voice replied, "But you are female." Thistle lied with accomplished proficiency. "I have been working for myself and find that some elderly ladies prefer a woman to a man. They feel... more secure. That's how I get the work."

"Okay," said the gruff voice. "Come along tomorrow afternoon and we'll see how we get on."

'Don's Decorating Services' operated from a corrugated iron shed in the garden of Don's house on the edge of Bistead. The business consisted of Don, the balding, endomorph-shaped owner, his wife, who 'did the books', and a core group of operatives. "I get a lot of insurance work," explained Don, sat across from Thistle at his messy desk. She had been instructed to sit on a plastic patio chair.

"We have quite a lot on right now, but one of my chaps has just fallen off a ladder and broken his arm in two places, so I need someone who can start straight after Christmas." He pulled at his jacket cuffs and brushed his lapel as if to convey his importance.

"Well, I'm just the girl... err, I mean, man that you need." Thistle beamed with confidence and zeal. Don took a deep drag of his cigarette and, eyeing her with a mixture of suspicion and amusement, had the thought: *If I say she*

*could be an assistant then I don't have to pay her as much as a man.* He cunningly calculated his weekly saving.

"One week's trial. If you are rubbish, then off you go. You can start 8am on Wednesday 2nd of January."

"I have a scooter to get me to the job."

"No need. Mick the Greek will pick you up in a van and then you'll be ready to help him unload equipment and paint."

"Thank you, Mr…"

"Mr Don – that's what the lads call me – and said with respect."

Thistle stopped at the phone box to report to Ruth the good news and check the arrangements for Christmas. She had no qualms about failing in her new trade; if her skills needed polish then her charm did not.

"Thistle, why don't you come over on Christmas Eve? We are walking up to the Duke of Wellington for a few bevvies. Jed has sorted out the spare room. It's crammed with all our craft materials, but you can kip there on a camp bed."

After Ruth put the phone down Jed exclaimed, "Why are you so kind to her? She's a nutter."

"She's an orphan, Jed. I chose the life I have; she didn't choose hers."

Thistle was relieved to escape the house on Christmas Eve; Kitten would be at her parents, therefore Steve would be looking for a rampant frolic with a Christmas fairy. Saddle bags packed, she scooted off to the city. Fortunately, the weather wasn't the same as it had been one year beforehand; it wasn't snowing. The Duke of Wellington was once a

coaching inn; it had two saloon areas. In the smaller public bar local bikers played pool and darts. The large lounge had recently been redecorated and replica military collectibles were strategically placed to create atmosphere. Thistle sat at a table with Ruth, Jed and their friends. They were the youngest of the clientele, who were mainly older couples sat in groups, and widowed or divorced ex-servicemen propping up the bar.

At eight o'clock the canned Christmas music was turned off and the publican made an announcement: "Sorry, folks, but I've just heard that our dear old friend Bill has fallen off his perch. Dead as a dodo, so we have no live music tonight – not unless there's a pianist in the house…"

Thistle had not noticed a honky-tonk piano in the far corner of the room; a blanket of cigarette smoke had enveloped an alcove lit by candles. "Go on," said Ruth, who had visited Thistle when she was with Ronnie and remembered their piano. As if in one of her imaginary stories Thistle found her way to the piano, adjusted its stool and began to stroke the keys with her still very stumpy fingers. Seasonal melodies cut through the fog, drifting into the ears of sedentary celebrators and generating a far more authentic atmosphere than the phoney collectibles. She paused only briefly to swig on glasses of cider ornamenting the top of the piano; people showed their appreciation. The evening flew by; eventually last orders were called, and Thistle stopped to demolish the rest of her free drinks. There were too many, so she gifted two full glasses to Ruth and Jed.

As the three were about to leave the publican touched her arm and shoved five pounds in her hand. "You deserve

that. The oldies stayed later than usual. I'll give you seven pounds to play on New Year's Eve. What do you say?"

Cash registers popped up in her eyes and suddenly the future was looking much brighter. She did not want to ask Ruth for another overnight stay and suddenly an idea crept into her mind. "Of course, I would love to, but I cannot possibly down all those drinks as I will have to scooter home. If I bring a cap, could you indicate 'pennies in the hat' from the punters instead of booze?"

The publican was also a quick thinker; he made money on all the drinks bought for a piano player. "Yes, but in that case I can only pay you another fiver."

Thistle shook his hand. "A deal."

New Year's Eve mimicked the previous Monday evening. The audience, with an average age above fifty, were thankful that someone could entertain them with all the familiar 'old tunes' that Bill used to play but deliver those songs with much more professionalism. Thistle's shrewdness paid off; there was much more than the difference between five and seven pounds in her 'hat', which was a beret that Ronnie's mother had given her a previous Christmas. Ruth and Jed had gone to a party with people of their own age. Thistle allowed herself a couple of whiskies at the end of the evening. "To help me face the evening chill," she said to the publican as he counted out five one-pound notes. He did not ask how much the beret contained; he respected her talent and that she had made a wise move.

"You brought in more than the usual number of customers, even for New Year's Eve. Bill used to play for beer, but as long as there's a full lounge, I will pay you to play every Friday night – five pounds a session." To make money by doing the thing one loves is a rare experience for most people, and a vast improvement on being obligated to perform an act one hates to achieve the same outcome.

At 8am on Wednesday 2nd January Thistle was appropriately clothed in her scruffiest garments. Right on time Mick the Greek pulled up in a white transit van with the logo 'Don's Decorating Services' streaked across its side panels. Black hair and facial features confirmed that Mick was indeed Greek. He could speak perfect English but had no intention of talking to Thistle; he could not understand why the gaffer had employed a girl. Once parked outside 'the job' he reached into the rear of the vehicle and threw a set of overalls at her. "Will these fit?" she politely enquired.

"Should do – they were Paddy's, the Irish, an ex-jockey. The legs will need rolling down a bit."

"What happened to him?"

"Rounded up after the Guildford pub bombings of '74. Never heard any more… come on – no time for chat."

Mick the Greek was a highly skilled plasterer. A water leak had caused damage to the very fancy living-room walls of a pricey property on Bistead's rural boundary. Part of one wall required a complete re-plaster; Mick attended to this whilst Thistle was assigned to remove the peeling wallpaper from a 'feature wall' that had dried out during the interval between the seepage occurring and December, when the insurance company had eventually instructed Don to commence work. Later on Mick told her to 'first coat' a wall that had not been so badly affected. Thistle was as nimble with her paintbrush as she was at climbing up and down the ladder. Mick was determined to find a flaw. She was resolute that he would not succeed in this. The battle for supremacy continued for the rest of the week and into the next. By late afternoon a week later the 'job' was completed. Don requested that Thistle stop by at his office-come-garden shed.

"Mick is a hard task master, and he isn't keen on modern ideas – like employing a female."

*Tell me something I don't know*, thought Thistle.

"But he reckons you have done alright, so this Friday you are due nearly two weeks' pay, after that your wages will be weekly... that's if you still want to stink of paint and scrub your fingernails until they drop off."

"Oh yes, I mean, I do... all of it. Thank you, Mr Don."

Thistle was always exhausted by Friday evenings but found a new lease of life as she scootered over to the Duke of Wellington to meet the needs of a group of ageing crooners, and satisfy both her financial necessity (Don's pay was a pittance) and yearning for musical expression. It was on the third Friday evening in January that the publican spoke to her before she commenced playing.

"My cousin has a pub over your way. It's the other side of Bistead down at Ashbrook, near the estuary – the Anchor Inn. He says he would like to hear you play. Can you go tomorrow? His piano is better than this one and he reckons he could give you a regular slot on a Saturday night."

Thistle's letter to Ronnie contained no detail, only that from the end of January she would be fully self-sufficient. She had just returned from the post-box when she came across Steve loitering by her door. "Thistle, my little poppet. Are you ready for another rent reduction?"

"Sorry, Steve, but your 'little poppet' has a little, teeny-weeny speck of... disease." Steve looked at her with scepticism, but he knew he couldn't risk proving himself right.

As 1980 progressed Steve's pursuance of Thistle acquired a tone of subtle intimidation. "Enjoy it in the back of that van, do you?" "Spreading your legs again today, Thistle... I think I am first in the queue." "What's it like up against a ladder... my bed is soft, warm and just waiting for you."

Thistle was aware that Steve would lurk outside the bathroom or behind the front door to accost her. She ignored his lewd comments, which served to inflame him more. Steve could have rescinded her tenancy, but that would have been self-defeating; he had taken a sip of her sexuality which left him intoxicated and frantic for more. Kitten's attraction was her youth. In many ways Thistle exhibited an equivalent appeal, and this excited him. She had the same under-developed body and a suggested vulnerability, but unlike Kitten Thistle was accomplished in the art of seduction.

There was no sex with Don's operatives. Eventually Thistle worked with the rest of them, not just Mick. The younger ones were annoyed that Don had employed her: "Men's work and it should have gone to a bloke." A couple of older men who had worked for Don for years were looking forward to retiring and couldn't care less about her or that Don had employed a female. Thistle did not have to charm anyone; using her technique of observation she identified unspoken custom and practice: Don's quote to an insurance company would estimate the time a job would take. The operatives never needed as long as quoted but once in a property the householder would invariably ask them to take on another job for a 'back-hander'. Don took a cut of this; everyone was happy. Thistle's rank was only ever as 'Assistant Operative', therefore she did not reap a penny, but her knowledge of this con guaranteed that the men gave her no trouble. Don came to consider employing her a good decision; with her assistance the operatives completed jobs even quicker, enabling more 'cash in hand' work on insurance company time. He also discovered that she had not been wrong when she said 'old ladies' liked a female operative, even though at the time that had been a fabrication. Thistle enjoyed the variety of working in different houses and once the weather was spring-like she assisted with outdoor assignments, which was even more agreeable.

So too was playing piano on Saturday evenings at the Anchor Inn; the piano had a finer resonance than the one at the Duke. The pub lounge was of similar size but very dated. Dulled, early 1960s, botanical-inspired, lime-green wallpaper and a nicotine-stained ceiling were horrifically contrasted by sun-bleached, olive-green curtains and matching beer-stained chairs, many of which needed a complete re-upholster. However, the pub clientele were a cheery bunch of middle-aged locals who consumed plenty of alcohol when singing along to Thistle's repertoire of classic ballads and timeless songs. It was her twenty-third birthday on Saturday 15th of March. Neither the publican nor the customers knew. In fact no-one knew anything about her other than the publican's description: "A pretty young thing... comes in on a Saturday night and she can't half play the old Joanna." Thistle had a plethora of lies rehearsed should anyone ask questions, but she had no cause to use them. No-one asked; no-one took any notice. Most of the time all they saw was the rear view of a head and its wavy, ice-blonde hair. All they heard were hauntingly nostalgic renditions of their favourite music. Her privacy was protected and both publicans continued to pay five pounds. The beret collected a similar amount and Thistle's income was further augmented, but not enough to fund renting a different bed-sit away from Steve, his obscenities and insinuations. It was in mid-April that she noticed Steve's disappearance; his Cortina Mark 111 had not sat on the driveway for days and sexual frustration did not monopolise the hallway.

"Where's he gone?" she asked the introverted man from the other room.

"He's a loan shark. Didn't you know?" he replied, condescendingly. "Gets into shady business... then has to hide away. Don't worry, he'll be back."

# 5

# Kismet

A FEW DAYS after Fliss's twenty-fifth birthday two cards arrived from France. Alain's was teeming with words of love. Jerome's simply said, "Bon Anniversaire, Fliss." *Of course*, she thought, *the strong, silent type*. If only Fliss could decide exactly what type of man suited her. She had tested various models whilst carousing city nightlife, but 'Mr Right' continued to elude her, and the quest in itself had become more focal than the result. Fliss had written a couple of letters to Alain and Jerome, and sometimes thought about phoning them. She wouldn't ask to use Hilary's phone for calling abroad: *I should use Mum and Dad's*. Yet, she never asked to. Her mother and her grandmother had married Englishmen, therefore 'he' must be out there, just waiting to find her. Hence why Fliss needed to be visible in places where males congregated – pubs and clubs. After Hilary's sordid experience with the predator from Bertie's Fliss decided that venue was unlikely to harbour her sort of man. She persuaded the girls from work to meet at alternative locations; there were plenty on offer. Equally, there were plenty of men on offer. Originally Fliss thought that she would sample them in her bedroom at Hilary's but was dissuaded from this plan by a growing mixture of regard for, and protectiveness of, her landlady. *I cannot compromise Hilary's values and I won't complicate her life or her home.* As the weather warmed up an occasional beau would visit to sit in the garden and chat over a beer, but he was never invited to stay overnight. Hilary took marginal notice; she was busy piling soil around the small- and medium-sized pieces of an early 1950s dispensed with bath, to produce her long-planned rockery.

One day in late May Fliss sat in a deckchair lapping up a martini and lemonade while watching her. "Hilary – I know that it was awful for you with that monster at Bertie's, but you haven't given up finding the chap of your dreams, have you?"

Hilary took a few moments to study her; she had learned that Fliss was adept at asking 'trick questions'. "Fliss – I believe that the more you look for something the further it will be hidden from you."

"Blimey, Hilary, that's a bit deep."

"In addition, unless you have a realistic picture of what your dream will be, then you will not know where to look or whether you have found it." Hilary's enunciation was that of a Vicar delivering a sermon.

"Hilary, have a martini… it might lighten your mood!"

Hilary roared with laughter; she always loved those rare moments when her dry humour got the better of Fliss.

"But you know, Hilary, what you say makes sense. I'm always searching, impatient, hankering after something, someone… and it is perpetually just out of reach."

"Like a butterfly," mused Hilary, as a red admiral pirouetted past on its flight to a patch of aubretia, tumbling from a boundary wall.

"And I don't even know what my butterfly looks like, do I?"

Hilary nodded. "Neither do I. Perhaps all the butterflies have been netted already – after all, you are now twenty-five and I soon will be."

"Will you? When?"

"Early June."

"We have to celebrate that, come on, what date?"

Hilary knitted her brows. "Sunday the 8th, but I have to go home."

"Hilary, this is your home."

"You know what I mean. Dinner with Mum and Dad. It is expected."

Fliss gave one of her bottomless sighs that habitually emerged at the mention of Hilary's parents. "Saturday the 7th then. I assume that clubbing isn't high up the list of suitable ways to mark your special day, so I will cook you a scrumptious meal and then we can walk up the pub."

"That dive?"

"You have only been in the off-licence. I and… never mind… well, I have had drinks in there with a few of my fellas. It's got a nice atmosphere – old-fashioned. Will suit you down to the ground!" Fliss hollered in triumph; she had won this round.

❧

Hilary had to work on Saturday June 7th, but Fliss did not, which allowed her plenty of time to prepare a pre-birthday feast. It was a very warm day; she would usually have been found sun soaking in Hilary's incomplete garden, but by this epoch of her life Fliss had learned a modicum of how to be unselfish, and after a shopping trip to Bistead she set to work. On Hilary's return she was greeted by a strong smell of apples and garlic. "Everything is ready, Hilary… it is mainly the traditional cuisine of Normandy, but the wine is from the Loire."

Hilary's feet had swollen in the heat of the bus. She shook off her sandals and accepted a glass of Touraine Sauvignon Blanc. Imitating Fliss's renowned 'curled-up lips' style of smirk, she enquired about the array of dishes. Fliss outlined the menu as the pair sat down to hors d'oeuvre against the backdrop of a nomadic breeze roaming in through open windows and rustling its pleated, block-print, coffee-coloured curtains.

"To start, we have homemade country-style pork terrine served with olives and slices of garlic baguette." Hilary looked at the terrine with a smile of admiration. "I am very impressed."

"To follow will be Poulet a la Normandie, which is two poussins, browned then braised with apples in calvados and cider. They are served with a cream sauce made by using the juices. To accompany will be fine French beans and Normandy potatoes, which are cooked with bacon and bacon fat. Dessert is Gateau au Chocolat, also made by 'moi', which is popular all over France. Bon appetite!" Fliss had produced a fine banquet for two with the assistance of ingredients from Bistead's recently established Saturday French market.

To drink with the poulet she produced a bottle of Bourgueil. "This red wine is made from the cabernet franc grape, grown in the same area as Alain's father's vineyard."

"Are you missing Alain? Or that other one?" Hilary tasted the wine, which was light in flavour and very palatable.

"Oh, I don't know. We are back to that old conversation; how do I find 'The Impossible Dream'?"

"That's a song, it comes from *Man of La Mancha*, a musical."

"You know a great deal of random facts, don't you?!"

"The result of working in a library. We loan out LPs and tapes as well as books."

"Do you loan out men?" Fliss puckered her lips.

"No, but libraries do accommodate men, you know, especially intellectual ones."

Fliss chortled. "No good for me then. What would I find to talk to them about?"

"Fliss, you could talk to anyone about anything!" The laughter that followed was evidence of friendship between two exceedingly different people who had come to understand and accept each other.

"Presents." Dinner was finished and Fliss insisted on clearing up whilst Hilary prodded the piano keys. Attempting to play any of the 'Five Short Pieces' by Lennox Berkeley after a few glasses of wine was doomed to failure.

"It isn't my birthday until tomorrow…"

"Have them now, I can't wait to see if you like them."

Hilary unwrapped the first: *The Reader's Digest Illustrated Guide to Gardening*.

"Oh, Fliss – thank you so much. Just what I need!"

"Now open the other. It isn't quite so sensible."

The next unwrapping revealed a trendy, cap-sleeved, voguishly faded blue denim shirt. "Try it on." Hilary did. She knew that Fliss had the best of intention but was uncertain whether the shirt was suited to her. Fliss read her face. "The perfect colour for you – and it's stylish without being brash. You look lovely."

Hilary was unaccustomed to the positive attention that she received from Fliss. She realised that she 'mattered'. It was a novel feeling. Hilary kept the shirt on for the visit to the Anchor Inn, the pub located just along the road from her maisonette. Due to warm southerly winds the pub doors and windows had been left open. She and Fliss turned left past the off-licence section, walking under the sign 'Lounge Bar'. As they entered a room in which the cigarette fog had been lifted by fresh air, the melody of Nat King Cole's famous song, 'Unforgettable', revived a drab, dated bar inhabited by clusters of time-worn patrons. The music arose from a corner but all Hilary and Fliss could see was the rear view of a young woman whose head was crowned with long, wavy, ice-blonde hair.

The publican and a couple of locals recognised Fliss from her use of the lounge bar for weeknight assignations. Purchasing two martini 'mixes' she joined Hilary at a chipped oak table. At that moment the music stopped, and the pianist turned around, her eyes picking out Hilary and Fliss as being the only other young people in the room. Thistle's face resembled a sunbeam on a sunny day; it radiated simplicity. If there was anyone that Hilary would have liked to resemble it would have been this vision, perched on a piano stool, smiling at her. In Hilary's eyes this was the most gorgeous creature that God had ever created. *Kallima Inachus – the most beautiful butterfly in the world*, she remembered a photo in a book. She did not notice Fliss's expression. As Thistle's crystal-blue eyes shone across the room Fliss felt a shiver run up and down her spine. Her eyebrows furrowed. *Neener, neener* – the sound of a siren shrieked a warning which ripped through her head.

"You play like an angel." Hilary had offered Thistle a drink; it was one hour later, last orders but not yet drinking-up time. Thistle did not hold out her beret, choosing to accept a half-pint of cider. It quenched the thirst acquired from performing on a stuffy evening. She was sat opposite Hilary. "I haven't seen you in here before…" Thistle's query sounded innocuous.

"It's my birthday… tomorrow. I live down the road… so we decided to celebrate here." Hilary's words floundered. She was transfixed by eyes which were penetrating her soul.

"We live together, down the road," added Fliss, emphasising the word 'together'.

"That's nice," said Thistle, sweetly. "So near to the estuary…"

Hilary immediately fished for common ground. "I try to play the piano, but I need sheet music. Your ability to play by ear is incredible."

"I have never thought of it that way," lied Thistle. "Do you have a piano?"

"Yes. It was my parents, but when I bought my own home they let me take it."

Fliss slapped her hands on her thighs in a gesture of 'end the chat'. "Well, I guess we had better get going, Hilary…"

"I could teach you to play by ear, if you would like…" offered Thistle, ignoring Fliss's attempt to steal Hilary away.

It is almost impossible to teach someone to play the piano 'by ear', for that is a natural gift which usually materialises in childhood. When Hilary remembered the butterfly Kallima Inachus, she did not recall that when it closes its wings its beauty vanishes and it merely resembles a dry leaf, thereby creating the perfect camouflage. Such butterflies are not easily netted.

Fliss hoped the interlude with Thistle would remain exactly that, a brief interval in normal life. Hilary obeyed her parents' directive to spend her entire birthday with them after their return from church. This was not for her benefit; they wanted to sort and label things for charity but were now too immobile to get up into the loft. As Hilary hoisted bags up and down a loft ladder it struck her that despite her parents having made countless friends through their church, when jobs required action it was her that they called on. Fliss made the unusual decision to visit her own parents. Her brother Philip and his wife brought the baby round. Fliss watched intently as the baby jabbed at its mouth with its finger then gazed with unadulterated love at its mother, secure that the person it was studying would protect it from all harm.

"You're very quiet, Fliss," observed Marguerite.

"Am I?" Fliss sounded wistful and her general conduct was completely the opposite to her usual modus operandi. Marguerite was momentarily perturbed, but then the baby threw up all over its mother. Marguerite rushed to fetch a cloth; the mother held her baby close and reassuringly purred into its ear.

*Love is so simple,* thought Fliss. *Why do I make it so difficult?* The next day during her lunchtime break, Fliss explored uncharted territory – the city library. She was relieved to find that Hilary wasn't on the lending floor; it saved an embarrassing explanation. Fliss headed for the section of books on psychology and 'self-help'. Obtaining a library card took longer than she had expected, but she was back in the department store just in time for the afternoon shift with three books hidden from view in a large tote bag. Fliss did not take to reading. Scrutiny of the literature on offer left her feeling slightly defeated, but that evening she settled on the sofa with the library books. Hilary had gone to the pictures with Sandra as part of her birthday celebration; Sandra had returned from a holiday with her husband the day before. By the time Hilary returned, the books had accompanied Fliss into bed.

Three days later, as Fliss drove them into the city, Hilary remarked, "Are you feeling poorly, Fliss?"

"No – why?"

"Because you haven't seen any of your entanglements yet this week and you have been oddly quiet."

"Work is so busy with the early summer stock take." (This was the truth.) "I am tired with working late every evening, and I have to work this Saturday without having had a half day off during the week."

Hilary was satisfied that her housemate was well. She did not disclose that she had arranged for Thistle to visit on the coming Saturday whilst Fliss was at work. Hilary had given Thistle her phone number before leaving the pub the previous Saturday evening. What struck Hilary as strange was what happened, or rather what didn't happen on Friday evening: Fliss did not spend hours in the bathroom preparing herself for club-land, although she had foregone the previous Saturday's night out to spend it with her. Perhaps as curious was that Hilary was the one monopolising that facility.

"I am going out with Sandra and her hubby – he is still home and it's the anniversary of the day they met." (This was also true.)

"Why do they want you hanging around on such a romantic occasion?" Fliss giggled.

"They haven't been back from their trip to Torquay for very long. I expect they've said all they want to – to each other!" Hilary also giggled. This was only partly true. It was Hilary's suggestion to Sandra on Monday evening that they all go out for a drink to celebrate the day Sandra met her husband.

"I have heard of a nice pub that has military connections," Hilary had explained. "It's near the city centre but not too far, the Duke of Wellington. He would like it in there." Hilary had lived with Fliss long enough to have picked up a little of her craftiness.

Fliss was glad of time alone. All week she had struggled to get past the chapter titles of her library books. This evening she decided to make a concerted effort. *Self-Analysis* by K. Horney sounded easy enough, but words like neuroses, psychoanalysis and rationalistic left her wishing she had also borrowed a dictionary. The second book she chose was *The Integrity of the Personality* by Antony Storr.

*I am full of integrity, and I have lots of personality, so this should hit the spot.* That had been Fliss's rationale for choosing Storr's book. Some of the chapter titles contained words such as 'introjection, dissociation, projection'. Fliss decided to skip straight to the chapter title that contained the words 'Heterosexual Love…'. This chapter seemed to suggest (from what she could understand) that to fall in love with a man she would have to 'identify' with females and also feel 'grown up'. *Oh boy*, she thought. *Of course I identify with girls. I go out clubbing with them all the time and I make friends… as I have with Hilary. Plus, I am grown up enough to hold down a good job, pay rent and not get myself into too much romantic trouble – so what more can I do?* She flung the book aside. None of it made sense. She liked the title of her third choice: *Sex in Human Loving* by a Canadian, Dr E. L. Berne. Every chapter was about sex, talking about it and talking about people talking about it, but once again the complexity was too intense to hold Fliss's attention. She looked at the back cover: *He's dead, like that Horney woman.* She suddenly cackled. *What an unfortunate name! But what good is reading stuff that must be so out of date? We have feminism now – what did they know?* She returned to the author still living, looked at the back page and realised that the synopsis talked about men and their way of relating. She slammed the book shut, walked to the kitchen, poured a martini and lemonade, and retrieved her latest edition of *Cosmopolitan* from the living-room coffee table. The books were returned to the tote bag. *I'll take them back to the library tomorrow; at least I know Hilary won't be working.* She was outside savouring her last Gauloises of the day when Sandra and hubby dropped Hilary off.

"They have a car now?"

"Yes, Sandra passed her test last month, so they have finally bought one."

"Have you had a good evening?" Hilary nodded.

Fliss continued, "As I am working late tomorrow to complete stock-taking I won't come back for dinner before clubbing; I can change at one of the girls' places."

Hilary's head resembled that of a 'nodding dog' – that tawdry statuette that some people put on the parcel shelf in the rear of their car. She was reluctant to speak further because she did not want to conceal anything behind words. Sandra and her husband had been impressed by Thistle's playing. Hilary had hoped that they could have stayed on once Thistle had finished, but Sandra was working a Saturday shift at Bistead library the next morning and keen to leave. All Hilary had the opportunity to say was that Thistle could arrive in the afternoon and have something to eat before she began playing at the Anchor Inn. Now she would not have to mention any of that to Fliss.

❧

Steve had reappeared in early May. At first he acted quite sheepishly around Thistle. She was inordinately keen to discover what trouble he had obviously brought upon himself, but it was imperative that she discourage his sexual interest, so she tried to keep out of his way and continued to search for alternative accommodation.

In late May Don took his wife on a six-week cruise. Everyone assumed that Mick the Greek would manage the business in Don's absence, but Don announced that Mick's responsibility would be for ensuring materials and equipment were up to date or on order. Operations Manager would be Neil. He was one of the younger operatives, ambitious, clever in a sly way and a clandestine misogynist. Once Don was safely aboard ship Neil called Thistle into the office. "I have been reviewing the accounts and can maximise Don's profits by streamlining workloads. I have reassigned jobs to utilise each person's skills."

Thistle had not been invited to sit down so shifted uncomfortably from foot to foot. *Surely he cannot sack me*, she thought.

He continued with no hint of emotion in his voice, "I know Don would not want me to let you go, but according to my calculations your current position as an assistant operative is now required for four days per week only. I will review this again in about three or four weeks. You can go."

Mick was not in favour of Neil's decision to reduce Thistle's hours, but men tend to stick by each other, especially in 'trades'.

This ended any hope Thistle had of finding a new flat. That late May evening was as inviting as a ripened pear, and the sunset stretched for miles. She scootered down to the estuary and stared at the horizon as if in a trance. A cruise ship was exiting the harbour; it wasn't carrying Don and his wife but in Thistle's eyes it might as well have been. *Protection – disappearing on a journey that I cannot follow.* As dusk fell a distant image of incandescent light began to glow, a star. Thistle's meditations were enticed by its stupefying shine, which reached out from diminishing sky-blue pink, occasionally framed by high, purple-edged clouds. She spoke aloud to the stellar celebrity: "Please – grant my wish. Send me the answer. I must survive."

On Saturday June 7th (Hilary's pre-birthday celebration with Fliss) Thistle began playing the piano in the Anchor Inn as she had done for over four months. Her fingers controlled the keys with little conscious effort on her part. Gradually over preceding weeks, Steve had begun his misconceived attempts at seduction. Her brain was rattling ideas like a well-shaken maraca. She wasn't sure what induced her to turn around from the piano shortly after the entrance of two young women, one full of spirited charisma, the other conveying the stillness of a dove coupled with shy discomfiture. Neither was she sure of what motivated her to seek their company.

# 6

# Attachment

ONE WEEK AFTER Hilary first met Thistle she was to be found in the kitchen preparing a Bolognese sauce, which was still the only recipe Hilary could successfully follow. Thistle arrived at three o'clock, not wanting to appear too eager. From the driveway she took in the external surroundings. The main door to the maisonette was on the side of the building, near to exterior steps. The building was semi-detached and of a rendered design fashionable in the early 1950s. Beyond the steps were two dustbins. Hilary was putting rubbish in one.

"How lovely, Hilary, you have a good-sized back garden, with an unusual medley of shrubs along the rear boundary."

"Yes, and the square of grass and flowerbeds at the front also belongs to me. I moved in during the winter and haven't had much time to make it all as I would like."

"I used to love gardening," said Thistle, remembering Eric and Vida's plot and her own that she tended when with Ronnie. She did not inform 'which' gardens.

"I have built a rockery, look, near the bottom but not in the shade of the shrubs. I haven't yet put in the plants I bought; they're like soldiers lining up against the shed."

"I can help." Thistle was perky and engaging. "Where is your lodger?"

"Fliss is at work – Williams and Brown department store, in ladies' fashions."

"Fliss? That's a strange name."

"It is actually Felice, it's French. Your name isn't common. Surely you were not christened, Thistle?"

"Karen. That's what I was christened." Something in Thistle's voice kerbed Hilary from asking about the name change. "Hilary, would you like me to help you with those plants now?" Thistle knew that teaching Hilary to play the piano by ear would be an uphill struggle. Hilary agreed with the idea of planting. The following day's weather forecast was rain all morning, after which she would have to go to her parents for dinner. The pair set to work, and snippets of information were spontaneously forthcoming, but neither divulged anything that wasn't superficial. Eventually Thistle entered the maisonette and met the piano whilst Hilary served up chilled soft drinks. "It has a good tone." Thistle confirmed Hilary's opinion with a run of her fingers. "Play for me, Hilary." Hilary pulled up a dining chair which served as piano stool. Nervously she played a few bars of sheet music: 'Easy Graded Mozart'.

"I had lessons as a child, did you, Thistle?"

"Yes." A dim memory surfaced: Thistle sat on her father's knee in front of a piano. He held the young child securely whilst one of her chubby fingers produced 'Baa Baa Black Sheep' by ear. "But I could work out tunes long before I had lessons. I must have been only two or three… lessons did not start until I was six but ended when…" Thistle stopped speaking. Once again Hilary intuited that questioning would not be appropriate. Thistle noted Hilary's diplomacy and continued, "In secondary school I learned theory and I used sheet music for concerts. A music teacher gave me some help… but I prefer to play by ear, I find it freeing."

"Yes, I can imagine that, because you can bring your own emotion to it… give yourself to yourself – in a way."

"Perhaps that's what I do, but when I play in pubs I have to offer up what people want to hear. I can't improvise or lose myself as I do when I play alone."

"What is your piano like?"

Thistle sucked in a breath. "I don't have one at the moment." That was the only significant fact that she had been forced to reveal. Her starting time at the Anchor Inn was seven o'clock. Hilary's spaghetti Bolognese was one of her better attempts, but Thistle did not eat all of her portion. "Sorry, I have a small appetite."

Hilary may have been slim like Fliss, hence why she could wear her clothes, but suddenly she noticed how thin Thistle was. Her clothing was loose and floaty, so often used to disguise excess fat but in this case masking an under-nourished willowy frame and limbs which protruded like the legs of a flamingo.

"Are you going to come up to the pub, Hilary?"

"No. I would not feel at ease sitting there alone."

"But you would be with me—"

"I would feel out of place… you don't see a woman on her own in pubs and that is what it would look like."

Thistle left in time to re-park her moped and place the beret in a prime position. Hilary wandered out into the garden to admire her newly formed rockery. Looking up she observed a darkening sky: *Altostratus clouds. The rain is arriving before morning.* And it did. Fliss ran from the car and hurled herself and two large tote bags through the front door. She immediately noticed a whiff of garlic escaping from the kitchen. *Hilary has been cooking. For herself?* Entering the kitchen she noticed two plates, two glasses and two sets of cutlery on the draining board. She quietly retreated to her bedroom, not wanting to disturb Hilary and whatever man might be in her room, although as she slid under the sheets she thought it highly unlikely that Hilary had company in bed.

Sunday saw Fliss not as bleary-eyed as normal. Hilary was at the breakfast bar, reading the Sunday paper with a cup of tea, when Fliss emerged and filled the cafetière. She was absently looking through the window into the garden and cried out, "Hilary – your rockery has plants in it."

"Thistle helped me," replied Hilary, without removing her eyes from the newsprint.

Fliss felt internal annoyance descending but steadied herself. "I guess that accounts for two sets of crockery and cutlery. Did you make Bolognese?"

Hilary raised her head. "Yes."

"You didn't say she was coming over."

"I didn't think I had to."

"I am sorry, Hilary, but I feel that there is something not quite right about her, that's all."

"Fliss – I agree with you, there is something 'not quite right' but that isn't about her as a person, however it may be about things that have happened to her. I don't know – but she deserves our concern, not our judgement."

"You are always so accepting. You literally do not see what is sometimes obvious. For example, you didn't see the black skin of that young chap, your 'first love', any more than you see the darkness in people's characters. That awful guy at Bertie's—"

Hilary cut in, "Fliss, I never question what you get up to, or with whom. I have music and gardening in common with Thistle. What do you have in common with all those 'fellas' of yours?"

Fliss was startled. Hilary had just hit an unspoken nail on the head. Her words had more impact than Hilary had expected. Fliss's face crumpled.

"Fliss – please let's not fall out."

"You are such a nice person, Hilary. I don't ever want our friendship to end. I will try to be kinder – to be more like you. And anyway – I am becoming bored with all my fellas. None of them are 'him'."

"Then stop searching."

Fliss's face brightened. "But what else shall I do?"

"Find a hobby!" Hilary pretended to wag her finger.

Fliss laughed. Tension was dissolved and a peaceable atmosphere restored.

❧

Thistle knew exactly where she wanted to be and the conniving that would be required to reach her destination. The chief obstacle was Fliss. Thistle thought it would be easy to poison Hilary's mind against her and divide the friends, thereby creating a spare room for Thistle to move into. The first piano lesson began the following weekend. Hilary worked fewer Saturdays than Fliss, so once again Fliss was working but Hilary was not. Thistle arrived in the afternoon. Hilary had made Bolognese sauce but this time enough for three. In contemplating Hilary's 'lesson' Thistle realised that to begin with it would be best to show her how to introduce a few improvisations into a piece Hilary could already competently play using its score. Hilary had enough ear for music to produce a reasonable sound but to play without any notation was beyond her.

"Sorry, Thistle, this isn't going well, is it? I am wasting your time. You must have better things to do."

This was not what Thistle wanted to hear.

"It will be slow, but you will get there – trust me. Perhaps it is enough for today. Why don't we go for a walk by the estuary?"

Thistle was always more relaxed when out walking. Responding to Hilary's talent for listening she began to open up. She described her years of living in a children's home, the security of Eric and Vida, the latter's sudden death, and the abandonment that she once again felt. When Hilary discerned that Thistle had reached a pause, she offered her own thoughtful reflections.

"As a youngster I used to sell 'Sunny Smiles' – booklets of individual faces – the babies and toddlers who all lived in National Children's Homes; it was a church-organised fund-raiser. I always felt it was wrong to display little one's photos – exploitative, I suppose. After all, did any of those children say it was alright to be on show? I don't reckon they even knew. Those unknowing smiling faces were probably not smiling at all in real life, were they? How terribly sad it must have all been. And for you, a tender eight years old when you were thrown into the care system… so very young… then to be placed in a bed-sit aged only sixteen. Shocking. But you are now twenty-three – are you still in the same bed-sit? Have you no family anywhere to go to?"

The subject of extended family was a scant discussion; Thistle's mother abhorred her relatives, and her father's kinfolk seemed to have disappeared when she was a toddler. Thistle faced a sudden dilemma about whether to disclose her life of recent years: the truth or lies? She stopped walking. Hilary stopped also.

"You have a very kind-hearted disposition, Hilary." A tear meandered down Thistle's cheek. The compassion of this acquaintance asking Thistle about herself was cutting through layers of intended deceit. "I am married… well, separated." The blurting out of the truth took them both by surprise. Hilary gently touched Thistle's shoulder and then a pair of arms circled Hilary's own shoulders, whilst a heavy head nestled itself into her neck. A memory of doing the same into Panda's neck sprung into Thistle's mind.

Fliss rushed in just as Hilary was dishing up. Thistle again ate only a little and the mood of the dinner table was that of speculation and unanswered questions, mainly Fliss's, but with Thistle present she had to remain polite. Fliss had made a significant decision that day: to dispense with 'clubbing' for a few weeks. To her work friends she explained this apparently aberrant behaviour as necessary to save enough money for a holiday with three of them to Benidorm. Two girls worked in children's wear so were able to book the same leave period as those in lady's fashion.

"I am not going out with the girls tonight, so if you would like to listen to Thistle play up the pub, Hilary, I will accompany you." Hilary was pleased. Thistle in a quandary: happy that Hilary would be there but annoyed at Fliss's magnanimity. When would there be an opportunity to push a wedge between them? Thistle had left when Fliss helped Hilary to clear up.

"Well – find out any more about her?"

"She has had a rotten deal – she's been discarded, deserted, bereaved and used as some kind of trophy wife."

"Good grief… well, I am going to be as benevolent as you are and make her welcome." Hilary did not reply. She was stunned at Fliss's change of heart and astounded that Fliss had the word 'benevolent' in her vocabulary.

Hilary's talent for listening was matched by Fliss's flair for speaking. As Thistle became a more frequent visitor, Fliss's idea of being 'welcoming' was to engulf her in words and food, assuming that Thistle would enjoy her vivacious vernacular and French-influenced menus. Hilary knew that Fliss was attempting to be kind but was both baffled and embarrassed by her non-stop, superfluous chatter, and as Fliss was still not 'clubbing' the only respite was when she was at work, meeting a man for 'casual drinks' (as Fliss described it) or visiting her parents. On those occasions Hilary and Thistle would play the piano, tidy the garden, go for walks or just listen to LPs on Hilary's Dansette record player. Their relationship was comfortable and unassuming. In mid-July Hilary's parents took off on a coach tour of Scotland. "They use these tours as a way of making annoying visits to my brother and sister!" Hilary tittered. "At last, a whole Sunday in peace," she added. Thistle had been hoeing and edging borders all morning while Hilary mowed the lawns. Now they sat in two deckchairs, each with a plated sandwich balanced on her lap.

"And Fliss is at her parents…" Thistle's words were coated in duplicity. She continued, "You and Fliss are completely unalike. Totally opposite, in every way. She cooks, prattles endlessly, gets bored easily, doesn't appreciate gardening, music or books, hardly ever goes for a walk and seems to be a bit of a sex maniac."

Hilary smiled but said nothing; she thought that Thistle was just being amusing.

"I am surprised that you took her on as a lodger… being so different."

"I remembered her from school but did not really know her. She was able to move in immediately, which was very helpful because I needed the extra cash."

"Do you think she will go back to France? To those lovers?"

"I don't know, why?"

"Because… I desperately need to find somewhere else to live, and you and I are like hand in glove."

Without admitting the pre-Christmas rent-reduction sex, Thistle described Steve's carnal coercion. "I'm scared," she added. "And since I have lost one day a week's wages, I cannot afford to rent another bed-sit. I know I could afford what Fliss pays you…"

Hilary was thoughtful. "But your boss – Don – must be returning soon. Hopefully he will reinstate your hours?"

"No," Thistle fibbed. "Mick has told me that there isn't much demand for work at the moment." She swallowed, as if to suppress more dishonesty. Had she pitched this 'sale' right? Even if she had, the removal of Fliss would take more than highlighting her dissimilarities to Hilary, or exaggerating Thistle's own situation. A painted lady butterfly landed on Hilary's plate. It rested for a few seconds and was gone. She looked towards Thistle, who noticed confusion in Hilary's eyes. "Let's go for a walk."

As they strolled along the shingle path Thistle slotted her arm through Hilary's.

That night Thistle lay awake, tossing and turning. Her scheme to move in with Hilary was now of utmost importance and the reason was no longer purely about escaping Steve. *A soul mate doesn't have to be of the opposite sex. In fact, I don't want sex as part of any relationship, just love. Like I loved Vida. Sex is sleazy, squalid and hideous. Men repel me; their disgusting obscene habits, their grubby probing…* Her thoughts reached an abrupt standstill. Thistle remembered her reflection in the hallway mirror at her parents' friends' house. She was wearing a mint-green summer dress emblazoned with poppies and her head was a mass of ice-blonde curls, but before she turned away to make her escape she noticed that the eyes were those of a different child – a petrified neophyte in an inexplicable world. Karen had gone to collect 'dressing-up clothes' that the woman had promised her, but the woman wasn't there. Her husband was in.

"The dressing-up clothes are in a bundle, just here, on the floor..." he said as he led Karen into the living room. She had knelt to have a look when a hand pressed lightly on her back. Then there was a weight overpowering her, stifling, suffocating, pinning her to the floor. Next was that reflection; it reappeared more clearly – the little girl had flattened ice-blonde curls and her mint-green dress emblazoned with poppies was rumpled. *I will never know.* The memory was as buried as the purple bloom of a thistle amongst its barbs and spikes. How many people would pluck a bloom of such splendour if it were not surrounded by organic fortifications?

Don returned from holiday and was annoyed to discover that Thistle's hours had been cut. He also identified discrepancies which resulted in Neil being 'let go', as Don explained it to the operatives. The business had plenty of work to justify Thistle's role, but by now, in her head, she was adamant that the only place she wanted to live was with Hilary. She intimated to Hilary that although she had the extra day's work again, Don had introduced a new wage system that still left her out of pocket. Another falsehood involved Steve. Something had happened in his relationship with Kitten. He had moved on to an eighteen-year-old of dubious scruples who kept him entertained; he had dropped his pursuance of Thistle, but she did not inform Hilary of this. Hilary gave her a key. "If you feel threatened you can escape to here, even if we are at work."

The Thursday in August before Fliss's weekend flight to Benidorm, Hilary was working late but Fliss managed to skip off early; she had ironing and packing to complete. She was surprised to find the front door unlocked and a nasal permeation of aromatic spices suffusing the maisonette. *Hilary must have left work early... but cooking?* Thistle was in the kitchen, 'Fliss's kitchen', surrounded by pans and packets.

"What on earth are you doing?" she questioned, clearly cross at finding an invasion of her domain.

The reply was delivered with an aftertaste of icing sugar: "I thought that if I made dinner you would have more time to get ready for your holiday. You work so hard, Fliss – you deserve a night off from the oven."

Fliss pursed her lips. She knew she was being hoodwinked. It took every ounce of maturity for her to return Thistle's wry smile. "Very good of you, Thistle; I do have a lot to do. And what is that concoction which is stinking the place out?"

"Curry – authentic. From the Punjab. My ex-mother-in-law taught me."

Fliss disliked curry as much as she deplored Thistle's current control of her culinary throne. *I must be kind – like Hilary is*, she thought as she pushed open her bedroom door. *Thank God I'm going on holiday.* As it turned out, her thanks were rather premature.

Just as Thistle could play the piano by ear so she could play 'life'. Improvising: making it up as she went along, being 'in tune' to create a melody and adjusting the tempo or altering the rhythm. Hilary never learned to play by ear; she needed life's score to tell her what notes to play next, but in her relationship with Thistle it was as if the sheet music had been swept away, leaving Hilary unable to connect with the composition of realism. Fliss's temporary absence increased Thistle's enduring presence. "Why don't I move in to keep you company?"

"I don't think it would be right for you to have Fliss's room..."

"Of course not, but I could sleep on the sofa. It would give me respite from Steve..."

For Hilary the piano keys had become a jumble of notes and chords. In her mind the only melody she could hear was that of bewilderment and uncertainty. Thistle arrived with a small canvas bag on Sunday evening. In the middle of the night she tapped on Hilary's bedroom door. "Your sofa is not as comfy to lie on as I thought. Can I join you?"

Hilary had a double bed. Thistle knew this. She remained on her 'side' of the bed, but Hilary could feel her breath. Thistle was up with the lark organising Hilary's tea and toast. "See you this evening, Hilary." Thistle scootered back to her bed-sit where Mick was picking her up in his work van. "Mick, can you pick me up from Ashbrook for the rest of the week and possibly longer?"

Hilary felt furtive all day. She had shared her bed with a female. Then she remembered herself as a young child, when she would climb into her elder sister's bed for reassurance. She reflected on those faraway days. *It's no different, is it?*

Thistle returned before Hilary and prepared dinner. After watering the garden they listened to music. Thistle sat close to Hilary. "I really care about you, Hilary, but not in a 'funny' way. You know what I mean, don't you?" Hilary's eyes were blank. She no longer knew what anything meant. In many ways she wanted to be Thistle, to have her talent and prettiness. To have her courage and her audacity. Thistle continued, "We can be soul mates. Share our lives, our mutual interests… a home – all of that. Then we will both have the feeling of belonging." She sensed a tightening; Hilary said nothing. "Unless you don't want my company. Just tell me to go and I will. I wouldn't hurt you for the world."

At last Hilary turned her head towards Thistle and spoke. "I enjoy your company, very much. And I am also fond of you, but I am not certain of how that would work for us, you and me. Fliss has only gone for a week… what will she say? I don't think you can go on living here. It is too problematic."

Thistle was deflated but unwavering in her intention to take control. "Why don't we see what Fliss's reaction will be?" She took Hilary's hand in her own as one would if guiding a blind person along an unfamiliar path. Hilary needed musical manuscripts. Thistle had volumes of those in her imagination.

Fliss was lying on a sunbed under a parasol. Benidorm in August was too hot, even for this sun worshipper. Her friends were reading paperback novels; two had romantic yarns and the third was engrossed in a Stephen King horror story. They were all mates, but Fliss did not feel particularly close to any of them. *Perhaps that is the nature of groups*, she ruminated. Benidorm itself was a place she had decided never to return to. The evening entertainment of flamenco dancing exemplified the same shallow level of passion as Fliss had felt for any man since leaving Normandy. The nightclubs were stripped of finesse but sated with seediness. However, the geographical distance from her life at home permitted Fliss to analyse it from the outside. *Goodness knows what I am doing in Benidorm, but it is only for a week. What am I going to do with the rest of my life?* Fliss constantly had a notion that she was somehow in the wrong place at the wrong time. Her tendency to boredom was because of her anticipation that in the next moment everything would fall into place, and she could not wait for that to happen. *The more you look, the less you find; that's what Hilary said. I wonder what she wants to find. I assume that all any singleton wants is to get married, but I am not sure about her and now I am not sure about me either. Maybe I am fated to be a spinster. Oh no... please not that.*

Fliss could lie still no longer. She wandered off through Benidorm's hotel-dominated streets to the suburbs, the home of markets, artisan shops and native haunts. Reproduction Gucci and Fiorucci clothing and accessories dripped from stalls. Genuine leather items could be cheaply bartered for. She sat at a café, shaded from the singeing sun by its canopy, and ordered an iced coffee. *No pavement parlours or iced coffee in England. No whiff of freshly cooked fish either.* Across a nearby square a long queue was building for paella, which was being constantly stirred and served from an enormous, wide-bottomed pan. "Local cuisine," called out the chef, attracting tourists and residents alike. *Local cuisine*, repeated Fliss as she tasted revitalising iced coffee and savoured its lingering flavour on her tongue. It was the first she had enjoyed since leaving France, where café culture also thrived. She would sit at a café in Pont-l'Eveque, coffee in one hand, a Gauloises in the other. She closed her eyes and recalled the restored half-timbered buildings with their brown or duck egg-coloured shutters, and the church of Saint Michel where one branch of forbears, including Grandmamma and Amelie were buried. The family farm was a short way from the town. Many more people toured the area nowadays as part of their trips to visit the Normandy beaches, cemeteries and memorials; Pont-l'Eveque catered for an assortment of visitors. Fliss enjoyed iced coffee every day until the end of that week and with each sip a kernel of inspiration was swallowed.

She arrived back at the maisonette at one-thirty on Sunday morning, having first taken one of the other girls home. Fliss left the Renault in its designated parking space to be as quiet as possible. As she heaved her suitcase down the driveway she noticed a moped. At first she thought the upstairs neighbours must have bought one, then she recognised it. Tiptoeing indoors she immediately sniffed a mixture of garam masala and Cachet scent: *Odour of Thistle.* Opening the door to the living/dining area she expected to find Thistle on the sofa; it was empty, but on the coffee table lay a book, a biography of Judy Garland. *Thistle's choice of reading material – dramatic actresses with chaotic lives. Perhaps her moped has broken down.* Fliss was too tired to consider any alternative and quickly fell into a deep sleep. It was through blurry eyes that she heard the commotion of Thistle clattering mugs and plates. She fell back to sleep to be awakened once again, this time by the whirr of a small engine. Nevertheless, slumber overtook her. It was just after one o'clock in the afternoon when she fully awoke and came across Hilary in the kitchen. "Was Thistle here?"

Hilary looked bashful. "Yes."

"What, all night?"

"Yes."

"But where did she…" Fliss stopped.

"It isn't what you think. I would not have allowed her to have your room and she wanted to get away from Steve."

"So, this isn't a permanent arrangement?"

"I don't know." Hilary was hesitant. She had been on the verge of leaving to visit her parents and had therefore been caught unawares.

"Well, I do know!" replied Fliss with authority. "It will not be."

"But, Fliss – you don't understand—"

"No, I do not. I have no idea what your relationship with her has become and this is your property, so you can do whatever you like in it, but I cannot co-exist with her on a daily basis. Quite apart from anything else there is one bathroom. Do you want me to pack up and go?"

Hilary ran into the lounge area, threw herself on the sofa and sobbed into a velour cushion.

Fliss sat down beside her. "Oh, come on, Hilary – your mascara will stain the fabric."

"I'm not wearing any." The whining continued. Fliss felt dreadful and lost for words.

Hilary regained her composure. "Of course I wouldn't ask you to leave. I wasn't sure what your reaction would be… in fact, I am not sure of my own. I feel so sorry for Thistle, she has experienced extreme hardship and disappointment."

"But you don't have to be her rescuer."

"Maybe not, but I can't be another person who abandons her, and in any case, she fills a massive gap in my life. I concede that the three of us living under one roof could present problems. What if I said she could stay over on a Saturday evening after she plays at the Anchor? None of us work on Sundays so there is plenty of time to share the bathroom."

"Yes, that sounds perfectly reasonable."

Fliss kept her next opinion to herself. *What is not reasonable is that you have allowed her to fill that gap – your need for intimacy, which has not yet been fully explored within an authentic relationship with a man. It doesn't necessarily mean that you have any innate feelings for her. I wonder whether she realises this.* Fliss had remembered something suggested in one of the library's psychology books. This insight caused her to question her own needs and motivation: *Perhaps I do have some growing-up to do.*

The solution did not sound 'reasonable' to Thistle. The biography of Judy Garland was aggressively pulled out of the canvas bag along with clothing and toiletries. They now lay strewn across a single bed. It had been later on Sunday afternoon that Thistle met Hilary for a walk along the estuary after Hilary returned from her parents. Hilary explained about the logistics and Thistle had a realisation: she would not be moving in. Now it was evening, and the bed-sit walls shuddered at her anger. Panda cowered. Despite Hilary's attempts to reassure Thistle of her continued warmth and affection, Thistle heard only words of rejection. This separation from the object of her attachment was a stone-sharpened sword slicing through her dignity and right to subsist. *I don't exist*, was the message repeating itself in her head. A full bottle of whisky sat on the counter. On Monday morning Mick found a note pinned to the front door of the house: "Sorry – ill." On Tuesday she walked to the phone box and informed Don that she should be well enough to work on Wednesday. The whisky bottle was empty by then.

# 7

# Fliss

THISTLE DID NOT contact Hilary until Wednesday evening. She phoned from a call-box and twenty minutes later arrived with a bunch of flowers for her.

"What are these for?" said Hilary, noting dark circles underneath Thistle's eyes.

"To thank you for allowing me to stay last week."

Fliss had begun to suspect that Thistle never had an honest and genuine reason for anything but sucked in her lips and disappeared to her room in contemplation of how she could manage Thistle's presence without losing her temper. Thistle suspected that it was Fliss's influence preventing her from living there. The result of this tacit conflict was a tension comparable to the height of Mount Everest.

Thursday evening Thistle was back. It was warm outside, so she and Hilary lost themselves in the garden.

Fliss watched them for a while and felt an ounce of guilt. *It's not for me to judge. They are happy – perhaps that is all that matters.*

"Bank holiday this weekend," said Hilary when they came inside.

Thistle piped up, "So can I stay Saturday, and Sunday nights as there will be no work on Monday 25th?"

It took only seconds for Fliss to forget her charitable thoughts; she began to formulate a plan. She had already made arrangements for this Friday evening, but the following Friday Thistle would again be performing her regular stint at the Duke of Wellington; Fliss decided that rather than clubbing, if she stayed at the maisonette without Thistle in attendance, it would provide an opportunity to improve her own relationship with Hilary. "Next Friday I'll knock up something special for us, Hilary," she called out, loud enough for Thistle to hear.

*Drat*, thought Fliss when Thistle's face showed no emotion, *I am supposed to be growing up and now I am behaving like a child.*

The August bank holiday weekend weather was unusually fine and Fliss made the most of end of the season, sunbathing whilst Hilary and Thistle gardened or walked along the estuary. Thistle did not stay on when Hilary made her Sunday parents' visit. One of Fliss's fellas phoned to ask her out but she declined; she had no impetus to engage with yet another macho machine. On bank holiday Monday Thistle insisted on preparing chicken masala. Over dinner conversation was wooden and Hilary looked glum.

*Thank goodness we are back to work tomorrow*, thought Fliss. On Thursday she had a half-day off, but Hilary had to work late. Thistle had forgotten this and turned up straight from her work.

"I know that you don't like me," said Thistle. She was stood in the kitchen doorway.

Fliss was marinating two steaks. "It is not that I dislike you, Thistle, it is just that I care very much for Hilary, and I do not want to see her hurt or… used."

"Why would I hurt or use her?" Thistle was mentally stamping her foot and could not disguise the energy of that.

"Well… Hilary is always kind and thoughtful—"

"*Unlike you!*" Thistle spat the words, having decided that open confrontation was the only way to win this battle of wills.

Fliss was shocked. Ignoring Thistle's slight against her, she continued, "As I said, I care about Hilary and—"

"But I love her. Hear that, Fliss? I love her and I won't let you create ill feeling between us." The ill feeling was of course what Thistle was determined to create between Fliss and Hilary.

Fliss threw a paring knife into the sink. Her honey-brown eyes flashed in anger and in that moment she completely understood the French phrase 'crime passionel'. Fortunately there was a propensity of English blood running through her veins, hence why the knife was safely in the sink.

Reaching inside her fighting spirit to locate calmness, Fliss forced a measured reply: "I have no intention of creating ill feeling, Thistle – don't be so infantile. My concern is simply that neither of you are left damaged or forsaken because it appears that both you and Hilary have experienced enough of that in your lives. You and she can enjoy these steaks – they just need three minutes each side. I have to go out."

Fliss pushed past Thistle, grabbed her car keys and drove to a phone box; she did not want Thistle to eavesdrop on her call. She rang the chap who had wanted to see her the previous Sunday. He was keen and she needed a distraction.

Hilary did not mention the altercation. Fliss assumed Thistle had not told her, so kept quiet. Hilary had made plans to see Sandra on the Friday evening that Fliss had offered to cook something special.

"Sandra is expecting. Isn't that wonderful? She is so happy."

"Yes," replied Fliss with the enthusiasm of a snail. *Everyone is happy*, she concluded, and decided that as Hilary would not be at home, she might as well go to the city; nightclubs were a diversion on the roadmap of potential futures. Fliss was no longer 'hulk hunting', but bopping the night away left her too exhausted to care. She met her friends at Captain's Cabin; it had become their regular venue, although all clubs offered the same scenario: booze, loud music, dancing and a very outside chance of tangible romance. The famous song thrush was still warbling:

> *"Night world voyaging. The bar and dancefloor call me.*
> *Can anyone see through me? A connoisseur of carousels –*
> *a ghost among the crowd."*

The words began to nag at Fliss.

On Saturday when Fliss arrived in from work she told Hilary that after clubbing she would be staying at a friend's house overnight. Her fictitious explanation was that the friend had just broken up with a bloke and needed company. Fliss was unsure of where she may end up that night and had not needed to make any excuse to Hilary, but she was teeming with guilt, not quite understanding why. Thistle was tinkering at the piano in readiness for the Anchor Inn; Fliss kept out of her way. The truth was that Fliss was weary of her visits and even more mistrustful of her motives. Thistle's presence heightened a general feeling of disempowerment in Fliss. Life seemed to have been blown off course; she had never felt so far from its helm. The nightclub was as noisy and hectic as ever, and the familiar popular hit was obviously a regular choice of the DJ.

> *"Night world voyaging. The bar and dancefloor call me. Can anyone see through me?"*

*That damned song*, thought Fliss as she downed another brandy mixer, and in that moment Fliss began to see through herself.

That is why at two o'clock the following morning she drove out to the forest and used a key Marguerite had given her to gain access to her parent's house. At breakfast time Marguerite found her asleep on the sofa. She stealthily left the room, ushering Paul, her husband into the kitchen. "Leave her to sleep – she looks wrecked."

A while later Marguerite heard Fliss call out, "Mum – have you got any painkillers?" Marguerite dutifully arrived with a glass of water and two paracetamol. She sat next to Fliss, who was cradling her head. "I'm so sorry, Mum, I'm just so…" Fliss began to cry. Marguerite hugged her daughter, who blubbered between chunks of unintelligible dialogue. Eventually Fliss recaptured articulation.

"Anyway – I'm really sorry, Mum. I was always such a little madam when I was growing up… giving you all a hard time, throwing tantrums, refusing to do anything I didn't want to, pressing your buttons whenever I had the chance. How did you put up with me? Why did you go on loving me?"

"Fliss – it's what mums do. From babyhood until forever, mums will always love their children."

Fliss sniffed. "You're wrong, you know. I don't mean that nastily, it's just that not all mums are like you. Hilary's mum is at best neglectful and at worst unkind. But Thistle's mum abandoned her. How terrible was that? Their mums haven't loved them – maybe that is why they are…" Fliss sighed.

"Has something happened?" asked Marguerite.

"It's okay, I just feel a bit mixed up and I want you to know that I am grateful that you have gone on loving me – no matter what I have done… or do."

"And your dad – he loves you too." Fliss looked at her mother with an expression of incredulity.

Marguerite expounded, "He has always loved you."

"He has never shown it… he only had time for the boys, particularly Philip."

"Fliss, you pushed Dad away. He tried to get close to you, but you would run off shouting nonsense about not being our daughter. You used to say that Philip and Simon weren't your brothers. Dad was really worried about you. He was concerned when you insisted on leaving home aged only seventeen to share that flat in the city. He was constantly agitated about your decision to move to France. I think he was relieved when you moved in with Hilary, but now he is secretly disconcerted that you have arrived here in this state. He loves you, Fliss, and your brothers love you too." Marguerite's speech was enough to cause yet more tears.

"Where is Dad?"

"In the dining room building a matchstick ship."

Fliss jumped up. She slowly opened the dining-room door. Paul looked up from the dining-room table, a dry dock for his miniature vessel. He was astonished to see her tear-streaked face; for Fliss to cry was unheard of. She walked over to his chair and unexpectedly encircled his neck with her arms. "I love you, Dad."

"And I love you, Fliss… what has brought this on, eh? I'm sure we can sort it out… make it better, whatever it is that's wrong."

Marguerite had arrived just inside the room, quizzical about this change in her headstrong daughter.

Fliss groaned, "It is me who needs sorting out. I have been resentful for so long, believing that you didn't love me. I have unintentionally expressed that bitterness by trying to reign over each man I meet. I haven't really loved anyone yet because I have penalised them for being male. I have simply used men as fodder to nourish my self-esteem."

Her parents looked confused, but for Fliss these words, which crawled out from an abyss of profundity within her, were a revelation. "No wonder the moment my ardour wanes I feel bored. I am never interested in getting to know a man for his personality. He is just another victory."

Paul was embarrassed to hear this level of detail from Fliss but, looking towards Marguerite for guidance, permitted Fliss to continue uninterrupted.

"It's all falling into place, so I know what I must do."

"And what is that, dear?"

"Can I use the phone? I want to contact Didier about an idea I have had. I need to discuss it with him. It means me returning to France – you don't mind, do you?"

Fliss looked at Paul and Marguerite with a grin. Bright eyes, bushy-tailed, firing on all cylinders. *We have back the Fliss we know and love*, thought Marguerite.

"Staying for roast dinner?" she asked.

"Yes, please, Mum. I'll have a coffee then go and ring Didier."

The maisonette was devoid of sound when Fliss arrived back late Sunday afternoon, having discussed her ideas not just with Didier but also with Paul and Marguerite. Hilary did not return from her parents until nearly seven o'clock.

"I am this late because I had to help them prune the shrubs," Hilary grumbled.

Fliss cast her eyes up and down. "That's just too much, especially when you work all week and have your own garden to manage."

"Yes, I know, but I am having a week off from next Saturday. Tomorrow Thistle is asking her boss for the same week. I think we will easily get a bed and breakfast booking somewhere in September. So, we won't be around – you will have the place to yourself." Hilary touched her nose with her finger, giving Fliss a 'knowing look'.

"Hilary, it is probably best I tell you now then."

"What?" Hilary frowned.

"I will pay my rent up to the end of September, but I will be moving out as soon as I can stop working for Williams and Brown. I am handing in my notice tomorrow. I have calculated how much paid holiday I am owed and think I will only have to work for the next fortnight. Well, I am going to ask to finish then even without pay. At least I know you won't be left in the lurch because Thistle can have my room. You might want to let her know so that she can give notice on her bed-sit."

Hilary was aghast. "*No* – I never wanted you to move out. We have had lots of fun together; I didn't mean for Thistle to—"

Hilary had not finished before Fliss butted in, "It is not because of Thistle, or you or anyone – except myself. You were right when you said that the more we seek the less we find, so I have to construct a different lifestyle. It is time to be an adult."

"But why do you have to leave your job and move out? You can adopt a different way of living staying here."

"No, I cannot because I need to return to Normandy, to the farm."

"To Alain or that other one?"

"Neither Alain nor Jerome. I am sure they are with other girls by now, not that I care. You said find a hobby, well, I am going to turn my favourite activity into a business – I hope."

"I don't understand… dancing? Are you going to become one of those exotic belly-dancers?"

Fliss laughed. "No, of course not. Cooking – with a focus on local Normandy cuisine. A café-bistro. If I start it on a small scale in the autumn for the locals of Pont-l'Eveque and build up trade for Christmas, I should be established ready for next year's holiday season. I am thinking of setting up a campsite as well; more English people than ever before are bringing caravans over on the car ferry. The continentals are driving along the auto routes from the Netherlands, Belgium and Germany. I have spoken with Didier today; he says let's see how it goes. I have nothing to lose, do I?"

"No, Fliss, but I do… I lose you. Just as it seems I lose the friends I care most about."

"We will stay in touch."

Hilary had heard those words before.

"I know what you are thinking, Hilary, but I will keep in touch, I promise. I will write to update you. Actually – you could come over."

"No, I couldn't be that far away from Mother and Father… if anything happened."

"But with recent road improvements Pont-l'Eveque is now less than forty minutes from Le Havre." Fliss gave up; she knew Hilary wouldn't budge. "Let's have some wine and cheese and I will tell you all about it."

Hilary agreed to wine and cheese; this was obviously going to be one of Fliss's elaborate explanations. Fliss described the Cenier family and their farm. Great-Uncle Claude had suffered ill health for some time, so Didier was running everything. In Fliss's absence his pregnant eldest daughter and her husband had moved into a farm estate stone cottage, the one that Great-Aunt Amelie, and in past years Grandmamma, had lived. This left vacant a smaller cottage where the daughter and husband had previously lived. It was adjacent to the farm shop, an ideal site for Fliss's proposed café-bistro. It had a large downstairs area which could hold at least six large tables. It also housed a good-sized kitchen, cellar and living quarters for Fliss upstairs.

"It's a place where my wider plan can start."

"But do you want to be cooking all day?"

"To begin with I will provide morning coffee and patisseries, also mid-day meals; the French love their leisurely lunches. Locals regularly visit the farm to buy cheese, meats, cider and, of course, Calvados. That's an apple brandy which the Ceniers have been distilling for generations. I will need to find someone to wait tables, but if that goes well then perhaps nearer Christmas I might open it on Friday and Saturday evenings. It all depends upon the revenue and who else I will need to employ."

"You are a great chef – but don't you need to be trained?"

"My hero Michel Guerard initially learned from his mother and grandmother. Well, my mum is a crappy cook, but my grandmamma was superb. It is not just my name that I have inherited from her – I think cooking is in my blood. But knowing me, I will become bored at some point. My idea is to start the business up and, once I can justify it, expand. By then I hope to have persuaded Didier to let me convert one of the disused barns into a full-size restaurant, which will need the services of a senior chef. After that I can focus on developing a campsite. The farm has plenty of space. So – there it is. In a nutshell."

Hilary almost dropped her wine glass as she rocked with tipsy giggles.

"In a nutshell – one of your sayings, but it is always a coconut shell! They say 'dream big' and you are certainly doing that. You won't have time for men!"

"No, my dearest Hilary – I most definitely will not." Fliss reproduced the 'curled-up lip' smirk for which she was ever famous. "But the Picasso *Le Moulin de la Galette* poster print you gave me will be hung pride of place on the main wall, a permanent reminder of you."

※

Fliss negotiated a leaving date of Saturday September 13th. During the first week in September she was too busy making plans and sorting through her clothes to be bothered about Thistle's visits. Thistle herself remained non-committal about Fliss's impending disappearance just in case it didn't happen, but she delighted in giving notice on her bed-sit.

Steve took the news with suspicion. "Where are you off to?" he sneered.

"None of your f-ing business," she retaliated. "And I am not leaving a forwarding address." She communicated her new details by phone to Ruth and in writing to relevant organisations. She also wrote of the change to Ronnie in case of any legal matters, although the decree nisi wouldn't be granted for over a year. Don gave Thistle the following week off and Hilary booked a guest house in Swanage from

Saturday 6th. Fliss was relieved that Thistle kept her Friday session at the Duke of Wellington; she and Hilary could have a final evening together.

Fliss tested a new recipe which consisted of a broth made from seafood, butter, cider and crème fraiche. She served it with her current party piece: lyonnaise potatoes. Hilary was dubious about the seafood broth, but the flavour was refreshing to her palate. Dessert was a traditional apple tart made to Grandmamma Felice's own recipe. "Sadly, having worked today I can offer you only two courses, but there's still gooey cheese about to run away from the cheeseboard."

Hilary remained in awe of Fliss's cooking. "I am enjoying this like a condemned man enjoys a final cigarette," she commented. "From now on I am likely to be eating a wide range of spicy curries with rice, poppadum or naan."

"Well, learn to dish up more than sausages, fish-fingers and the rare Bolognese!"

"Yes, I think I might have to."

"I will leave behind one of my simpler cookery books. Mum bought it for me when I first left home aged seventeen, so it is easy to follow. There are recipes from around the world and for any occasion. *Five Hundred Recipes*, it's called. I will put it in the kitchen."

"Thank you. I may even try some of them out…"

"Write and tell me how you get on. I will also leave behind the full-length mirror; I won't need that where I am going."

"There will still be farm hands…"

"With farm legs, farm brains and farm pongs!"

"I will miss your humour…"

"And I will miss your compassionate soul, Hilary – so please take very good care of yourself. And just in case you ever want to go to a nightclub or fancy restaurant, I will leave you a few of my more tasteful dresses… if you don't want them, I am sure a charity shop will, but I hope one day they will come in useful."

For the second time that week Fliss found herself crying. She resisted offering up any further opinions about Thistle. Hilary was surprised at Fliss's tears and made an admission: "When I was young, I refused to cry. I held on to my grief, believing that in doing so I was guaranteed not to feel sadness, but as I matured I realised that I wasn't avoiding my feelings, I was merely burying them. From then on I wasn't afraid of tears anymore." Hilary shared in the tear making.

Fliss was off to work in the morning. Hilary made sure she was up in time to bid her farewell. "Will you be gone by the time we get back from Swanage?"

Fliss outlined a general plan for her final week in England, which would end with a visit to her parents. She would not be seeing Hilary and Thistle before leaving. With transparent kindness she wished Hilary well. "I hope you have a relaxing break in Swanage."

"The parents used to take us there as kids. It isn't very exciting, but I like the antiquated atmosphere, and it has a reliable bus service."

"What time is your train?"

"I am meeting Thistle in the city station at twelve o'clock. We are both getting there by taxi."

Fliss gulped. The reality of life transitions had finally sunk in. Once again she reserved judgement about Thistle.

"Hilary, maybe it is time you learned to drive. It would make life so much easier for you."

"Yes – I have been thinking the same, especially as now I will have no respite from the blood-curdling bus ride to work!"

Goodbyes were said without much sentiment; that had been exhausted the previous evening.

On Monday 15th September, after disembarking at Le Havre, Fliss took pleasure in the drive through lush Normandy countryside, which rambled on, seemingly untouched by its dramatic history. Her route circumvented most of Pont-l'Eveque but passed Eglise Saint Michel. A country lane took her to the farm. Didier, a compact, well-proportioned figure of a man, his wiry wife and their three daughters were waiting to greet her; the pregnant eldest girl reminded Fliss of a sunflower in bloom. The younger two ran up to Fliss; secretly they admired her for past displays of loose morals. Francine, the seventeen-year-old, diminutive and dark-haired, whispered in her ear, "I don't want to keep attending college so Papa said I can help you get set up, assist in the kitchen and wait tables. The locals all like me!"

Fliss's face lit up; Francine was a version of herself at that age. Didier and Fliss had much to work out in preparation for the new venture. He was an astute farmer and businessman whose knowledge and experience were exactly what Fliss needed. That evening Fliss ate with the family, but beforehand Didier showed her the living accommodation above the kitchen and hospitality area.

"This is so that you have your independence. We still come and go like rabbits at the farmhouse, but if you require anything either Francine or someone else will be happy to help. I perhaps need to let you know that Alain has returned to his family's chateau vineyard as manager, and Jerome is courting a girl from the town."

"This time my only interest is in getting the business going, and Didier, I am really appreciative of your support and wealth of expertise. I will have no space in my life for men."

"Famous last words," he uttered under his breath as he left Fliss to unpack.

# 8

# Letters
# and Lies

FLISS KEPT HER word: Hilary received regular correspondence. The first letter updated her on practicalities that Fliss and Didier were encountering, including obtaining licences and permissions. Fliss would not have had the patience to overcome bureaucratic red tape, but Didier did, and as owner of the existing retail business it did not take as long as Fliss had feared. A consequence was telephone calls between Fliss and Alain regarding Chateau Veronique becoming the main supplier of wines. The conversation was polite, if a little stilted on his part because he was seriously involved with the daughter of a count. Fliss was light and jolly; she didn't care who he was entwined with as long as she got a good deal on the alcohol. The Cenier farm could provide all the cider and calvados required, but there were no local vineyards. The next letter contained photographs of the café-bistro taking shape. Its mottled grey stone walls were decorated with colourful bunting and wall hangings made of willow, reeds or wood. Red-checked tablecloths with matching serviettes enhanced a rustic theme designed around apples and cheese, which was cleverly suggested by complementary use of décor and accessories. Each table's centrepiece was a pottery jug of dried hydrangeas. One dry-lined wall was hung with photos of rural French scenes contrasted with café posters, amongst which *Le Moulin de la Galette* stood out as 'jewel in the crown'.

*No mention of romance*, thought Hilary, slightly bemused. A further letter abounded with words of wonderment and excitability; the café-bistro opened its doors as Fliss had planned – to takers of morning coffee followed by the laid-back lunch brigade. She and Francine were rushed off their feet and Didier was rubbing his hands; faith in his cousin Marguerite's daughter had not been in vain and good fortune worked hard for, could be enjoyed by all involved.

Hilary lay this last letter down on the sofa. Her eyes looked towards a writing pad and pen which lazily stretched out against the velour cushions, like a cat enjoying a dream about dead mice. She had sent Fliss a 'Good Luck in Your New Home' card which contained a few lines about how restful Swanage had been. Nothing more. Reading came as effortlessly to Hilary as listening; writing was as taxing as talking. *What should I say? Where do I start? I could tell her that Margaret Thatcher's economic policies are being blamed for the recession and growing unemployment. Or perhaps she would like to know about another attack thought to be by the*

*Yorkshire Ripper. No, Fliss never took much notice of current affairs.* Hilary had the whole evening to collate her thoughts; Thistle was at the Duke of Wellington. Rain was attacking the windows with uncustomary vengeance; a clement autumn had descended into the underworld of winter. "Persephone has travelled to be with Hades," remarked Hilary to an empty room. "I know – I will begin with the driving lessons." She described her surprise at finding driving a car so easy. She was having regular lessons plus Sandra had added Hilary to her insurance so that she could practise. Hilary's parents could have done the same but made petty excuses not to. Hilary's new reading materials were car magazines; she had decided a Mini would probably be best. Sandra's pregnancy was showing, and Thistle's friend Ruth was also pregnant. *Yes – that all sounds good.* Hilary was stymied; why did she need her words to sound 'good'? *I am not writing any lies.* The absence of dishonesty is no guarantee of candour. Memories of recent months, since Thistle moved in, flitted past like fireflies.

"Hilary, why do you need to learn to drive? A car costs a lot of money and anyway – where will you go? Your precious friend Sandra can take you to the cinema until she drops one. Then she won't be going anywhere for a while. I'll invest in a better moped so that you can sit comfortably on the back. You *do not need a car*." Thistle had been stomping around the maisonette when she vented her reaction to the news that Hilary had booked driving lessons. Thistle had continued, "And Ruth is up the bloody duff. What's wrong with these women? Before the sprats are weaned their husbands will be humping them for another. What a waste of life."

"What is?"

"Motherhood."

When Thistle was in this mood Hilary chose not to oppose her. Ruth was not in fact married, but that was a technicality. It mystified Hilary that Thistle's recurrent irritability began not long after she had achieved her goal to become the lodger. There had been a brief 'honeymoon period' quickly followed by Thistle displaying unpredictable irascibility. It could come out of the blue, about people or events, but with no discernible cause. Hilary knew that Thistle harboured animosity towards Sandra but wasn't sure why. Sandra must have suspected it, though, because she never came into the maisonette anymore. Driving practices had eventually tapered off and cinema or tea trips became less frequent; Hilary assumed that Sandra's pregnancy was the reason. Ruth had visited the maisonette a few times; usually Thistle had a use for her. When Ruth had appraised Hilary there was disquiet in her expression. Hilary had no answer for that conundrum either. The forthcoming births were never discussed again.

She went to a draw in her sideboard and pulled out the photos Fliss had sent her. Casting her eyes around, she remembered Thistle's insistence that the maisonette be given a 'make-over': "Once all the autumn gardening jobs are done, I can make a start on sprucing this place up inside. You cannot really like it as dull as this, surely? And those coffee-coloured curtains… they have to go. I can ask Don to loan me a small ladder and then at least some walls will be painted before Christmas."

That had been late September. December was now in its infancy and one of Don's ladders a permanent fixture in the hallway. Hilary had quite liked magnolia but acknowledged that Thistle's job enabled her to be in tune with contemporary trends. As Thistle had become occupied by decorating, Hilary thought she could help by cooking dinners. She had perused Fliss's cookery book and chose a simple lamb hotpot. Thistle had clutched Hilary's hand across the dinner table. "You have made a splendid effort, but it is a bit… tasteless. I am happy to do all the cooking, honestly… I don't want you getting stressed."

Hilary did not want to accept defeat. For her next attempt she had selected a recipe for meatballs. Suffice to say Thistle's taste buds conveyed their opinion, shown by the meatballs being ejected from her mouth. Thistle had picked up Fliss's cookery book and headed for the dustbin. Hilary grabbed it from her. "It cannot be thrown away – it belongs to her; she may want it back."

The rain ceased. Hilary stepped outside into dank night air. The moon was screened by clouds, but she could see well enough to light a cigarette, a Gauloises. That had been another subject of disharmony; in late October Thistle had found her puffing away whilst sat on an upturned, unused piece of bath once intended for the rockery.

"Jesus, Hilary. What the… smoking? For Christ's sake – when did this start?"

"I found a packet of Fliss's underneath the sofa, and I quite fancied one, that's all."

"I have enough of the smell of fag smoke from both pubs, and the tossers I work with. It lingers on my clothes and overalls – I can't stand it and I certainly don't want to come home to it."

Hilary was not keen to become 'a smoker'. Oppressively smoky bus journeys were once again torture, and she was saving hard for her first car, but occasionally a sneaky cigarette hidden from Thistle's watchful eyes brought a feeling of autonomy. Back indoors Hilary picked up her written sheet of news and ripped it into tiny pieces before stuffing them underneath a pile of peelings in the kitchen bin. She used mouthwash after brushing her teeth. Despite their discord Hilary would not sleep until she heard the rumble of a moped and knew that Thistle was home, safe and sound. Thistle made choices. Sometimes she slept in the spare bedroom; sometimes she wanted to be with Hilary.

"It's the night terrors… they keep me awake and I find it hard to be alone."

Hilary would eventually hear Thistle's breathing change; sleep brought an episode of equanimity but not for Hilary. Using the half-light from a roadside streetlamp, which invited itself in through a gap where the curtains did not meet, she memorised the pattern on her Artex bedroom ceiling.

The next day was a working Saturday for Hilary. During her lunch break she bought a picture postcard of the city's civic centre and wrote four words: "*No news. Everything fine*," signing it, "*Love Hilary.*" The main post office was still open; the card was dispatched to France. On her return from work she was not greeted by wafts of spice. Thistle dished up shepherd's pie.

"I think you might be fed up with Indian food, so I made you good old English grub," said Thistle, brightly. She continued in the same carefree manner, "I was thinking that we could go and choose wallpaper for the bedrooms next Saturday, plus new curtains and cushions for the living/dining area; you do like the peach walls, don't you? I did ask you before I chose that colour, didn't I?"

Hilary couldn't remember so agreed that she must have, then she made the sudden decision to join Thistle at the Anchor Inn. Most of the locals knew that Thistle was now Hilary's lodger which eradicated Hilary's unease about being in the pub. The Anchor Inn's air was dense with cigarette smoke.

*Maybe Thistle was justified to complain about finding that unpleasant reek upon me. Perhaps I have judged her too harshly*, thought Hilary, with ladlefuls of self-reproach. *There's no disharmony – I shouldn't be so selfish.*

The following morning Hilary received a surprise phone call from her elder sister.

"Hello, Hilly-bonks…"

"Monica, I am twenty-five not five years old."

"Yes, of course…" Monica's shrill laugh rang out; it sounded as if a throttled hyena was at the end of the phone line. "Hilary, when you go to Mum and Dad's today, they will tell you that we have invited them to spend Christmas and New Year with us."

"Crikey, Monica – have you had a visit from God? Or are the Scottish Presbyterians looking to convert Wesleyan Methodists?"

Monica laughed once more. "Very funny! No – our business is flying high so we can afford the train fare and I know they would like to see Peter's kids again." (Peter was Hilary's older brother who had married into a sheep-farming family and spawned a feral brood of children. Monica and her husband were property developers; no kids but stacks of cash.) "I am ringing because they have accepted the invite, and therefore we will also pay for you."

"Thank you, Monica, but I couldn't possibly come; I don't have many days off over Christmas."

"Couldn't you ask for annual leave? Oh, go on, Hilly, you have never been up here and—"

"Sorry, Monica. It is a very generous gesture, but it would be unfair for me to leave my lodger on her own."

"I thought she had family living out the forest way?"

"That was Fliss. She is in France. I have a new lodger now who has no-one, and she is a lonely soul."

"Hilary, do you know why I used to call you 'Hilly-bonks'? Because you have always been bonkers… too good, too sympathetic – too blooming humanitarian."

"I am none of those things, Monica. I am awfully selfish—"

Monica interrupted, "Underneath that serious, sombre librarian disguise, you are a sweetie. Is there nothing I can say to change your mind?"

"One day I will come… I promise."

"Okay. In that case I will send you a cheque for the train fare that we would have paid; you can put it towards the car you are saving up for."

Thistle appeared as Hilary put the phone down. "Good news, Thistle; my parents are going to Scotland for the whole of Christmas. We can do whatever we like!" Hilary did not mention added funding towards buying a car.

❧

Thistle also had a reason for joyfulness later in December, but it proved to be a double-edged sword. Don invited her into the office and over a glass of whisky offered her a small pay rise.

"Nearly a year you've worked for me, and you have taken some stick. Nowadays you aren't just painting inside and outside, and clearing guttering, but hanging wallpaper too. Old George says you are getting the knack quite well. Of course, you cannot be treated like my men, but I reckon you deserve a few more quid. Just one thing, though…"

"Thank you for the pay rise. What is the 'one thing'?" Thistle tried to remain unruffled.

"The men have noticed that you… how can I put this… that you never seem to have a boyfriend. And… I have heard them comment that, with you doing 'men's work', you might be one of those, err, you know… lesbo types."

Her poise was exceptionally difficult to retain. Inside Thistle a steam train suddenly appeared, hurtling itself around a circular track, its vapour shooting into the firmament, leaving behind a patchwork trail of white balloons. She took a breath. "I am horrified that the male operatives should have drawn this conclusion just because I am not promiscuous. Would they think that's what I am if I had offered to shag them all? No. So in a man's world the fact I have morals becomes a reason for prejudice and bigotry. Perhaps you would prefer this 'lesbo type' to leave your employ?"

Thistle could not have afforded to resign, especially because employment opportunities were becoming increasingly difficult to find, but she knew the importance of strategy: righteous indignation being this one.

Don felt backed into a corner. He had motive to retain Thistle; he counted her as a definitive 'tick' against a tick list labelled 'modern man'. She was also good value for money.

"I will have a word with them. They haven't 'lived' or travelled abroad like I have, so I am afraid their attitudes can be provincial at times. Now don't you worry, and I am sure that one day you will meet a nice young man, get married and have a little family. And for your trouble… take this." He offered her a one litre bottle of Bell's whisky, which, like all his whisky, had fallen off the back of a lorry.

*No, you aren't provincial at all, are you, Don?* thought Thistle, as she politely accepted the bottle with a genial smile. Whisky had become her drink of choice.

The maisonette was festively festooned, and the postie shoved Christmas cards through the letterbox. Thistle received one from Ruth and an official card from work, written by Don's wife. Hilary received far more, not just from immediate family but also a few ageing aunts, current and ex-work colleagues. However, she was most looking forward to the card which would bear a French stamp and postmark. It arrived two days before Christmas. After the printed greeting of 'Joyeux Noel' were just a few lines: "*Will write properly after Crimbo. Have been so busy – we opened a few evenings and had lots of custom but now Great-Uncle Claude is very poorly, so Didier is anxious. I am fine and dandy, hope you are too. Get around to writing to me!!! Love F x*"

Hilary had intended to write in the card she sent to Fliss. *The path to hell is paved with good intentions.* She castigated herself when the card was dispatched almost empty of text except for a seasonal caption and the words: *"All great here, love Hilary xx"*

In some ways life with Thistle had settled down, partly because Hilary acceded to her wishes but also because Hilary had begun to doubt her own ability to make decisions, so she delegated responsibility to Thistle. The cream background wallpaper featuring multiple miniature posies of strikingly blue cornflowers did enhance Hilary's bedroom and blend with existing gold carpet. Hilary's ill-fitting bedroom curtains were replaced by a pair in plain cream satin sheen. The recently painted peach living/ dining room walls were complemented by curtains also sporting a floral design of sage-green and peach against a white background; matching cushions completed Thistle's pictorial project. How could Hilary be dissatisfied when Thistle's choices were so perfect?

"You do like it all, don't you, Hilary? Once we get into January, I will finish painting the woodwork in my room, hang the wallpaper, then I will tackle the kitchen and bathroom. To be honest they could do with a complete re-plaster, and then being tiled, but that would cost a fortune. I have watched Mick enough to know how to plaster the roughest areas, then I thought I could use tile-effect wallpaper over the top. That will hide uneven surfaces."

"Tile-effect wallpaper?"

"It's all the rage for people on a low budget. Don't worry – it will look fab."

Hilary wasn't worried, well, not about the decorating. She was bothered by hiding the date of her driving test. After

Thistle's outburst about the lessons, Hilary had arranged to have them during her lunch break.

On Wednesday December 24th the library closed early. Hilary took a bus to visit Sandra and swap presents. Hilary felt contrite about Sandra but could not explain this to herself; images of Judas Iscariot would sometimes amble into her mind. Thistle honoured a commitment to play piano at the Duke of Wellington. The publican at the Anchor Inn wanted her too, but Thistle felt her first obligation was to his cousin at the Duke. In addition, it would be more lucrative; the number of coins thrown into her beret had been dwindling in both pubs, but the Duke being a city pub, attracted passing punters at Christmas who tended to be more generous. She wanted Hilary to catch the bus and join her, but she declined. Ruth and Jed would be there with their friends and Hilary was disinclined to have to socialise with them; she wouldn't know what to talk about.

Christmas morning saw Hilary and Thistle exchange gifts of matching woolly hats, gloves and scarves, chocolate, and toiletries. It was a frosty morning with an azure sky that brazenly boasted a bonny ball of sunshine, so off they strode for a long walk along the estuary. Thistle took Hilary on a narrow footpath that left the bank to weave its way through woods, eventually reaching a field which edged the harbour village where Thistle had moved to with Ronnie. She showed Hilary Ronnie's house, knowing that he would be with his parents. The front garden was overgrown. Thistle slipped down the side of the house to witness the rear garden in the same state. She made no comment to Hilary.

They wandered down a hill to the water's edge, where they sat on a bench watching lonesome boats fluttering on the tide. Snapping an elastic band of silence, Hilary opened a floodgate to untried waters: "Would you like to talk about how your marriage broke down?"

Thistle was awaiting that question; by showing Hilary her once village home she had instigated it.

"I didn't love him. Does that sound heartless?"

"What – never?"

"No, Hilary, not ever. I suppose I believed I could learn to love him because there seemed no obvious reason not to. Now I realise the truth."

"Which is?"

She looked at Hilary in the direct manner that Thistle adopted whenever she needed to present the case for her defence. "The reality is… that I can never love a man. Please do not be taken aback. It is very simple; I think I was interfered with… as a little girl, just before Father disappeared."

Hilary was more than taken aback; astonishment caused her mouth to gape. "You 'think' you were – or 'know' you were?"

A tear fought its way out from Thistle's fair eyelashes. "I cannot remember it all. Just glimpses, sometimes nightmares."

"Was it your dad?"

"Oh no, no – it was a family friend. I am sorry, I should not have shared this repellent memory with you."

Hilary held both of Thistle's hands in her own. "You have been severely traumatised. I don't know what to say… this is the most perturbing thing that I have ever heard. I feel privileged that you trust me enough to talk about what must have been a terrifying experience… and it helps me to understand you better. Come on, let's go home, hand in hand."

Hilary was not being truthful. As they retraced their steps all she could think about was how little she knew or understood Thistle. Child abuse was not a subject that Hilary had even read about. Her mind dwelled on how Thistle had dealt with something so appalling, and how much it impeded her ability to relate. It was another explanation for Thistle's so often tainted attitudes. Unable to process all of this, on that Christmas afternoon Hilary began submerging into a sea of perplexity, like a ship with a leak in its hull.

Fiddling about on one of the boats was a member of Ronnie's clique. He witnessed the interaction. A harbour-side pub was open for Christmas lunchtime drinkers. He made his way there, joined his compatriots and triumphantly announced, "I've just seen Ronnie's ex-missus. He was right, you know: she's a raving dyke!" They all laughed loudly as they bloated their bellies on cheap beer before staggering home to gobble the Christmas meal so lovingly prepared and presented by their compliant wives.

❦

Thistle's disclosure had a significant and healing impact for her: the night terrors stopped and although sleep had to be aided by whisky, once she had drifted off, she rarely awakened before morning. Her confidence in Hilary had been paramount. *Golden times*, thought Thistle to herself as January 1981 weathered a few snowstorms but proceeded into February with no upheaval. Continuous decorating was an uphill task; cutting tile-effect wallpaper to fit around the back of kitchen appliances, a toilet and cistern was immeasurably complicated, but Thistle tackled it like the rest – with gusto: *It is my way of thanking Hilary: my best friend, my soul mate. I am so lucky. After all I have been through, life has thrown me a diamond.* Hilary was as priceless as an unaffordable fragment of stone. She read Thistle's mind and could not bring herself to act in any way that may impair Thistle's faith. Hilary cancelled her driving test and used some of Monica's Christmas money to buy a radio-cassette tape player. However, the 'diamond' was not as perfect as Thistle would have liked.

"Hilary, why don't you have your hair dyed? It is rather an insipid colour – a darker tint would help to define your features… contrast with the lack of cheekbones. So too would metal-framed glasses; you would look so much better. And to help with your weight loss – you know you have gained a few pounds – I will serve your food onto smaller plates. You don't want to develop a bulging waistline, do you?"

❧

Just before Thistle's March birthday a letter from Fliss crossed with a letter that Hilary had eventually written to her. Fliss's writing rambled on, a caricature of her speaking style:

"And so it has all been really difficult with Great-Uncle Claude dying not long after Didier's eldest gave birth. I never knew that Didier's mum had passed away when he was only three and Claude became both mother and father. I think that's why Didier is so affected – they have been much closer than most men with their dads. My plans for expansion have had to go on hold. Didier has aged about ten years and says he cannot cope – he is even talking about hiring a proper manager for the whole business. For goodness' sake – that could throw a spanner in the works, but I am trying not to worry. Mum is coming over for the funeral; it's been delayed because of a post-mortem. Everything here is governed by regulations; Didier is due to inherit the business, but I know for a fact he wouldn't have murdered his dad! Now I am going to impress you – in the little spare time I have, I am improving my ability to read and write French. I learned how to talk it quite fluently the last time I was here, but writing down the grammar, with words being masculine or feminine, isn't easy to take on board. I have forgotten what I learned at school! Francine is teaching me; in return I am helping her improve her English. Also, Hilary, and this will surprise you – I brought some English paperback books here with me and Mum is bringing me more when she comes. I am a reader! I wish I could see your face – are you smiling or wincing? You may have guessed that the books are all trashy novels, not the intelligent stuff that you digest, but they stop me thinking about men. I know I said I wouldn't have time for them, and I haven't, but I can still have fantasies! Now you are pulling your librarian face – I know it. I am so *pleased that Mum is coming. She hasn't been here since Grandmamma's funeral. Do write soon and tell me about your driving. Have you passed your test yet? And how is the cooking coming along? Give Sandra my best wishes for the birth. Take care H, love F x"*

*Phew. It is exhausting just reading her letter. So apart from the fact that she now reads books, it doesn't sound as if she has changed very much.* Hilary chuckled at fond reminiscences of Fliss's exuberance and how infectious it could be. They had often squealed with laughter about the most ridiculous things. Hilary picked up *the Reader's Digest Illustrated Guide to Gardening*, in which she had recently been reading tips on growing clematis. Her eyes watered. Hilary wished Fliss had not gone away.

Fliss received Hilary's letter on the day before Claude's funeral. Marguerite was driving over from England and due to arrive late afternoon. Didier's wife had offered a bedroom in the farmhouse for her. Marguerite was intrigued by her daughter's appearance; Fliss emerged from the café-bistro, now named Le Pommier, with her silky black hair wrapped inside a dotted, red and white cotton headscarf. This hid the grown-out French-bob style which if set free fell into uneven layers, ineptly trimmed by Francine. The sleeves of a light-weight pullover were pushed up to the elbows. This and a pair of faded denim jeans were protected by an apron which matched the headscarf. There was no trace of makeup on Fliss's face; her skin shone like a well-polished apple. However, this face wore a puzzled expression. Mother and daughter embraced then Fliss proudly showed Marguerite Le Pommier, 'the Apple Tree'. After the tour Fliss led Marguerite into a courtyard area at the side of the building.

"I would like to create an al fresco eating area here with parasols or a canopy, a trellis with climbing plants and a few pots scattered around – what do you think?" (Marguerite had no chance to answer.) "We usually open Tuesday to Saturday, but I have closed it for the rest of the week out of respect. I also shut it for two days after Claude died. Francine and I have been busy this afternoon making savoury and sweet tarts for the funeral guests; they can have them in here tomorrow."

Finally, Marguerite and Fliss caught up on other news, then Marguerite asked, "Why did you look troubled when I arrived? You seem happy enough and I have to commend your efforts."

"I am happy and feeling positive about the future. I have stopped worrying about men, although I hope I meet my partner for life while I still have lots of it to live! The trouble is Hilary."

"Why? Is she unwell?"

"Read this. It's not just what she says but how she words it, and what she omits."

Marguerite read the letter.

*"Dear Fliss, I meant to write before Christmas but ran out of time. My parents went to Scotland, so for once I had a*

*Christmas during which I could do what I wanted. Sandra and hubby gave notice on their rented flat and are buying a house near his mum and dad in Taymouth. Her parents both work, whereas his mum doesn't and can help with the baby. It is due in April, so Sandra has resigned. I have not seen much of her lately; she is tied up with everything. I cancelled the driving lessons, there wasn't much point. It is expensive running a car, and we have a decent bus service. Thistle has been busy decorating the maisonette – it now looks up to date. Spring will soon beckon us into the garden. Have not had much time for cooking due to working longer hours; I am involved in inducting new library staff and have been asked to sit on a taskforce researching the improvement of systems. I am thinking of having my hair dyed and changing my glasses – I would be so much more attractive. Everything is going well. Look forward to hearing your news to date of 1981. Love Hilary x"*

"What is wrong with that?" questioned Marguerite.

"Oh, I don't know. My sixth sense telling me something. Mum, when you go home, could you arrange with Hilary to visit her?"

"But why on earth would I do that? She would think it odd."

"Before the funeral tomorrow I will buy some luxury chocolates. You can deliver them as a belated Christmas gift."

Marguerite's visit to Hilary, pre-arranged by a phone call, did not last long; it was a Saturday morning and Hilary had offered to help Sandra pack moving boxes. She had by then received Fliss's letter and offered her condolences on the death of Claude. She was thankful for the chocolates and for Marguerite driving all the way from the forest to bring them.

"It was no trouble," said Marguerite. "I had to pop into the city so was over halfway here. The maisonette looks very swish – you must love it." Hilary's reply conveyed no shred of emotion. Marguerite was careful not to outstay her welcome.

Earlier that morning Thistle had marched off to the estuary in a sulk. She was annoyed with Hilary for planning to help Sandra. Hilary felt that she had to defend her action. "She is a friend and heavily pregnant."

"It's her fault she's preggers and moving house. Anyway, you hardly see her nowadays, and once she is in Taymouth with a baby she won't be much of a friend to you, will she?"

*That should meet with your approval*, thought Hilary whilst keeping her mouth firmly shut. The chip on Thistle's shoulder was being forever more rigorously sculpted by the whittling of a character that neither Hilary nor Thistle knew the identity of.

Marguerite phoned Fliss later that day. "Well," said Fliss, "how is she?"

Marguerite hesitated, grappling with her own thoughts. Eventually she noticed something stood on the corner of a window ledge. "Fliss, I have just noticed a crystal vase in the window. I intended to buy some flowers for it today but quite forgot. Maybe because of Hilary. It is what she reminds me of – an empty glass vase. I could see right through to the other side because there was nothing there. Unoccupied. Vacant."

"Now I understand why her letter sounded all wrong."

"Fliss, there is nothing you can do. You are soon to be twenty-six and I guess she must be too. Old enough to make your own decisions and live with the consequences. I was already married and a mother at your age; my priority was family. Nowadays you young people have so much time and energy to spend on yourselves, so spend it wisely."

"But Hilary…"

"From what you say she is carving a career and apparently doing well. I am sure she will find her niche, just as you have."

When the call ended Fliss looked around at her creation, Le Pommier. *I have found a niche and you, Le Pommier, are my baby. There is one flourishing stem missing from my own personal vase of flowers but at least I have variety of colour and the perfume of elation. I do hope that a bouquet will soon land at Hilary's feet, and she will no longer be empty.*

# 9

# Romance and Renaissance

THISTLE DID NOT perceive Hilary's emotional detachment. Hilary's focus had increasingly become dedicated to the library, which at times irritated Thistle, but diligence did not equate with betrayal, so her barbs did not need sharpening. To the contrary, she used Hilary's heavy workload as the excuse to encourage Hilary to tell her parents that she could only attend for Sunday lunch on a fortnightly basis.

"Just tell them, Hilary. Jesus, they don't own you, do they? You have free will and you know that they use you."

Thistle's own focus was digging out wider borders in the rear garden ready for early summer planting. With every dig of her spade, she hacked through decaying roots of long-forgotten, redundant flora.

*These are relationships now starved of time and shared experience; inevitably they are decomposing into the earth.*

In her mind she was digging graves for the people who had vanished from her history and for those now disappearing from Hilary's. *She will come to understand that people will always evaporate into an illusion of how you wanted them to be. Ultimately, it's more rewarding to invent family, friends and platonic lovers.* Thistle's inventions occupied much of her thinking time. Tales of allegiance, gratification or utter desolation played out in her still-fertile imagination. Within these stories Thistle was safe from the threat she had most come to fear: bonding with living, breathing human beings. Her conceptualised creatures were always under Thistle's control, toys of mental manufacture. She decided their destiny; they could have no influence on hers. The pages of these narratives disguised their genuine author – the sculptor of her personality. The whittler. Her fragmented self. The fragmentation was exacerbated by Thistle's memory playing tricks on her, as she sought emotional cohesion. Her mother was now bawling as Miss Ramsey lead Thistle away. Her father had appeared on a winter's day, swept her up into his arms and promised that he would return; obviously he must have died. The staff at Chantry House used the term 'Princess' for Thistle and placed a tiara on her majestic blonde curls. Eric and Vida had specifically requested to foster her, having heard of her talent for playing the piano. She really was clairvoyant; she could read palms and she did know what lay ahead. Vida's death was all part of a celestial masterplan, as was her marriage to Ronnie. Situations and events once considered upsetting, tragic or regretful were rewritten with symphonic harmonies. Thistle stepped up to the podium as conductor. The orchestra of recollections followed her lead.

Hilary would observe Thistle concentrating on a page in a book, then notice that she had not turned that page for some time. A similar occurrence happened when they watched television: the screen was hypnotising to eyes which were not paying attention. Yet Thistle's piano-playing took on a dynamic impudence. *That's when she is fully in the moment*, deduced Hilary, vexed by Thistle's periods of withdrawal. She could not discuss any of this with her. Thistle's way of being was not subject of conversation; it joined a list of other taboo topics including: the library – if Hilary said too much about work Thistle began to feel inferior.

"You have a career; I am just a skivvy."

Fliss's name could not be spoken; for Thistle 'out of sight' meant 'out of mind', but under her skin there was a tingling – she felt that Fliss was closer than she wanted her to be. Babies: both Sandra and Ruth had birthed daughters. This caused consternation because Thistle did not want to be reminded that babies could be adored and girl babies would grow into quarry, hunted by men. Despite their common interests and affection for each other, Thistle and Hilary had metamorphosed into static cruise liners whose passengers had departed. Hollow vessels awaiting dry dock, manned by a skeleton crew. When life generates space, a natural phenomenon is for it to be filled – usually with something animal, vegetable or mineral.

If Hilary could be described as in the general state of stationary ship, then her work for the library service equated to being a tug boat – chuntering away, knowing its purpose, reliable, dependable and without expectations of grandeur. This tug-boat mentality had been noted by her seniors, hence the offer for her to widen her remit and embark on a path of training others. When she accepted this extra duty Hilary had not realised that the role involved travelling to all the suburban libraries. This often resulted in two bus rides to and from destinations, and hence elongated working time. She began to regret not having taken her driving test; increased remuneration she was now receiving would help to cover the costs of running a car. The additional undertaking was the taskforce that she had been commandeered to. By late May it was on its third meeting, and she had been asked to set up a tea and coffee facility in one of the civic centre meeting rooms (this building housed the library).

Hilary's boss explained, "A chap called Tony from International Business Machines is bringing the new electronic typewriter that we have purchased. It's a Selectric 'golfball' 3 – don't ask me what that means, but it is the latest model and has advanced features. He will give you all a demonstration. His main presentation will be about worldwide innovations in library lending services. He says that many American academic libraries and even a few in England are beginning to use electronic book issuing systems, rather than the Browne card-based method that we have known and loved for so long. I am sure it won't catch on, but they gave us a discount on the typewriter for allowing him to deliver his spiel. You must be my eyes and ears, Hilary. Do take notes and please clear up at the end."

Hilary was delicately arranging custard cream, bourbon and digestive biscuits on blue china plates; these seemed far more appetising than a dismal afternoon listening to a talk on technology.

Being so intent on this mission she did not hear someone enter the room until a male voice landed on her ears. "Hello, Hilary. I thought you were a librarian, not a canteen assistant."

She looked up sharply. "No – it cannot be…"

"Hilary, you have hardly changed – what is it now, six, seven years? And you could still pass as a naïve teenager!"

"I was expecting a rep named Tony." Hilary hastily adopted her assertive librarian manner.

"Yes, that's me. The name Charles sounded rather too 'country gentleman' for IBM so I abbreviated my middle name, Anthony. You never knew my middle name, did you? Actually, you weren't really interested in anything about me – and I was so eager."

Hilary was studying him as he spoke. His ginger hair was not the orange carrot top from her memory, having dulled over time to auburn, and his freckles had faded. A spherical face had slightly narrowed, and the beginning of laughter lines were evident running along his cheeks, almost reaching his chin. He reminded her of Andy Fairweather-Low.

"So," he continued, "I am guessing that you have climbed the greasy pole a bit and haven't been demoted to tea-lady. How's the family? Especially your mother – is she as grim as ever?"

Hilary's laughter echoed around the room like a peal of church bells. "Crikey, you have changed," she said between guffaws; this was not the Charles she had described to Fliss.

"For the better, I hope!" He was winking. "I remember your mother leaving us alone in your front room, but I am convinced that she was listening outside the door."

Hilary re-instated her librarian face. "I remember that you used to sound like a sermon and sing like a fog horn."

"Do you know that my practice of memorising the bible helped me develop the skill to deliver word-perfect speeches about a highly technical revolution which is starting to take place, even though for much of the time I don't understand a word of what I am gibbering about? But I still cannot sing!"

At that moment other members of the taskforce began to assemble, pouring themselves beverages and untidying the precisely positioned biscuits. Hilary did not care. She now had two hours to examine the man who in the past could not raise a smile in her but today had lifted her spirits with a belly-laugh.

After the presentation and a lack of sensible questions from the audience, Charles insisted on helping Hilary clear up. They left everything stacked on trays for the real tea-lady. "Did you enjoy the presentation, Hilary?"

Nothing of it had been absorbed. She candidly replied, "I didn't understand a thing. I cannot see this computerisation mumbo-jumbo getting much interest. We are also investigating the idea of a plastic token system that has been piloted elsewhere."

"The token system still requires some form of data storage—"

"And are you still touting for business Charles, Tony or whatever name you like to be called?"

"If it means I can see you again then I probably am…
and my friends still refer to me as Charles."

Hilary's cheeks felt flushed. "It has been pleasant to
catch up with you, Charles, but I have to lock up this room
and drop the key off at the kitchen."

"Do you fancy a longer catch-up, over a meal, maybe?
There's a good steak house opened up near the old walls."

"Charles, I really have to go…" Now she was flustered.
An inner voice sat on her shoulder like a pirate's parrot.
*How would Fliss handle this?*

Charles's speckled green eyes smouldered. "Sorry,
Hilary – short notice for this evening, I suppose, but what
about another evening – for old times' sake? How about
Friday? Are you still at home with the banshee of Bistead? I
could pick you up."

The parrot on her shoulder repeated the words. *For
old times' sake, for old times' sake… no harm in that, for old
times' sake.*

"Well… alright, why not. I would like to hear what your
sisters are up to nowadays. Friday would be okay. I live
in Ashbrook now." Hilary picked up a 'free' IBM pen and
notepad, and neatly printed her address and phone number.

"Is seven-thirty too early, Hilary?"

"Perfect."

This was Tuesday. By Friday Hilary was in a dither
and wished she had asked Charles for his phone number
so that she could cancel. She hadn't picked up one of his
business cards so had no way of contacting him. Her mind
was not on work. At lunchtime she phoned her parents;
they would have the number for his parents who would

know how to contact him. No-one answered the telephone. *Oh, bother*. She remembered that they were holidaying for two weeks in Littlehampton. She had kept the rendezvous secret from Thistle, yet on Hilary's return from work Thistle almost threw a plate of grilled mackerel fillet and salad at her. Obviously Hilary had not explained that she did not need feeding, but she speculated on whether Thistle had somehow discovered her tryst.

"What's wrong, Thistle? Has something upset you…?"

Thistle scowled. "The publican at the Duke of Wellington. He phoned just half an hour ago. It is his mother's seventieth birthday, so suddenly I have to be there early and play a banal list of her favourite songs."

"Is that so bad?"

Thistle began to shout, "Jesus Christ – of course it bloody is. I have my individual routine and I don't like it messed about with. I set the pace, the direction of what I do. No-one else. Oh – you wouldn't understand. You bow and scrape to everyone, toe the party line, keep to well-trodden paths and wouldn't stray further than a dog with arthritis. I'm off."

With those vicious words Thistle stormed out. Hilary walked into the bathroom and spoke to her reflection in the mirror. "Time to stray. Time to take the first steps on a different path." She diligently pulled the mackerel fillet apart and, ensuring it had no bones, gently tossed it over the wall at the bottom of the garden for next door's cat. Then she rummaged through the dresses that Fliss had left her along with the sandals she had worn on Fliss's twenty-fifth birthday night out. Hilary's feet had stretched them too much for Fliss's feet to feel supported afterwards. *Thirteen months ago. It seems an age.* She chose a knee-length, button-through black shirt dress that Fliss sometimes wore for work.

Charles could not have been more charming as he opened his car door, and Hilary, with a breath as deep as the Atlantic Ocean, engineered herself into the passenger seat without rucking up her dress. Conversation flowed like a babbling brook. The steak house was dimly lit, serving a sedate clientele; the couple's chatter was only halted by the consumption of mouthfuls of food. Nearly seven years of family intrigue and information was shared, plus chronicles of their own experience. He was impressed that she owned her own property and was a senior librarian with additional responsibilities. She was amazed that the gawky, awkward Charles, celebrated only for biblical renditions, had matured into an eloquent, entertaining and eye-catching man. *I wonder if he was once kissed by a princess*, said the parrot still residing on her shoulder. The fable of the frog prince caused another fairy tale to enter her mind, Cinderella. "I have to work tomorrow so I cannot be too late." (Subtext – she must be home before Thistle returned, especially this evening.)

Back at the maisonette he parked his car on the driveway. She did not invite him in. After commenting that darkness was providing a marvellous backdrop for the stars, Charles slanted his head towards Hilary's; her own mirrored the movement. Their embrace, as natural as the night sky, lingered with growing physicality. It was Charles who pulled away. "I am so sorry, Hilary." He sounded agitated.

"What for? It takes two to tango." Hilary surprised herself with such an uncharacteristic response.

"No – I shouldn't have let us get this far. It was wrong of me."

Hilary tidied her dress. "Charles, it's okay. I am nearly twenty-six. I am not that distant teenager, naïve or otherwise."

"I am married." The earth moved in a thoroughly different way than Hilary had expected. Charles blundered through an apology. "I wed Anna two years ago. I don't think you ever knew her. I thought your mother might have told you, but I realised that she hadn't. Anna's a nurse, works shifts, often at night. We just fell into marriage. My work for IBM means that I travel a lot. Sometimes we go weeks without spending quality time together. God – I don't know why I am telling you all this. Slap my face, Hilary. Make it hurt because I deserve it."

Hilary was never known for quick reactions. The parrot had flown off on the wind and Hilary had never missed Fliss so much. *She would know what to say, but I have to listen to myself, my wisdom, my heart.*

"Charles, I have had one of the best evenings of my life. I want to push you away, close the door on my feelings and never look back. But I can't. I want more, not less, and that is your decision. If you foresee that your marriage has the apparatus to survive then please shut, lock and bolt that door. But if in your heart you believe that your marriage has not the substance to persist, then you need to make other choices, be that me or someone else."

"I don't want to let you go, Hilary. I know that I must

work it all out. I am riddled with guilt about you, about her, but I need to see you again. Can I call around? On Sunday afternoon? She's working. Sorry – that sounds crass."

"Please phone before you arrive, out of courtesy for my lodger."

Once indoors Hilary poured herself a strong martini mixer. *Rocky roads ahead. Well, at least I won't be toeing the party line.*

The next day Hilary wasn't home from work for very long before Thistle had to start playing at the Anchor. There was no time to introduce the subject of Charles, and Thistle was still grumpy. Charles phoned at lunchtime on Sunday; he would be there at two o'clock.

Thistle's mood had lightened. "Where shall we go for a walk this afternoon? How about we head for Lady Sarah's Park? The rhododendrons will be full of flower. I know it is a trek, but there's no rush to get back."

Hilary leapt over a puddle of trepidation. "Sorry, Thistle – no can do. I have an old friend popping down about two. We will probably go off somewhere."

"Old friend? What old friend? Fliss hasn't returned, has she?"

"His name is Charles, and I knew him years ago. We were almost romantically involved and that may well happen again."

Hilary knew that she had lit the blue touchpaper. She stood well back and waited. Thistle was stunned. Her reaction was that of a wild animal who has been incapacitated by a drugged bolt, shot from an accurately aimed gun. All the years of control methodology sped through her mind in seconds. Feet remaining fixed to the spot and body rigid with tension, she opened her mouth. "How very nice for you. Okay – I realise that my words on Friday before I went to the Duke probably hit home more than you would care to admit, and you now feel the need to prove that a disobedient streak lies within you after all. I would never have thought you capable of game-playing, Hilary, but if you must embarrass yourself, go ahead. Knowing you as I do, your feet will slip off the side of the cliff; the descent will be bruising and no doubt you will expect me to be the one to catch you at the bottom – which of course I will. Then you can wrestle with the guilt and shame that follows you around like a neurotic puppy. Jesus, you are so pathetic and needy."

Hilary did not answer. In that moment all the aspects of Thistle that she had admired, aspired to, cared for and at one time worshipped, dissolved into invisible tears. *I put poison on a pedestal.*

From her bedroom at the front, Hilary could see the driveway. Charles parked his car in the on-road designated space and as he strolled down towards the side-on main door her heart skipped numerous beats. She couldn't remember ever feeling this way about anyone. Thistle reached the main door before her, and what a transformation. Dressed in her 'I am an ethereal elf' outfit, with hair flowing and eyes radiant with good humour, only the flower-head of a prickly weed was evident. She greeted Charles with grace and gentility and insisted that he survey the garden. Her manner was self-effacing but attentive. She asked him about his work and feigned some knowledge of technology. Once back inside she rustled up refreshing fruit cocktails whilst drawing his attention to her handiwork as a decorator. Charles was too polite to interrupt. He threw glances at Hilary, who could not climb over the fence of flirtation that Thistle was erecting at every turn. Time was passing and Hilary's patience wearing thin. She was ready for her chance, which arose when Thistle retreated to the kitchen to replenish glasses.

"Shall we go for a drive?" she asked.

"Please…" he replied. "Your lodger is a bit OTT, isn't she?" They were in his car driving east to find a remote venue for walking, talking and expressing the predictable desire of two people governed by primal instinct.

"Did you fancy her? Thistle, I mean."

"No way. Why do you ask that? You know who I fancy…"

"But she is stunningly pretty."

Charles drove the car along an asphalt track and pulled into a clearing hidden by redwood conifers. On occasions as an adolescent, he and a few undesirable friends, whom his parents had no knowledge of, travelled to these woods by country bus for the purpose of smoking marijuana.

"Hilary, I was always drawn to you. And do you know why? Because yours is a beauty which originates from deep inside. It glows with compassion and is embodied in every word you speak. It is not skin-deep or superficial."

"Oh, Charles… if only you had been so… so silver-tongued and flattering sat in my parents' front room!"

They kissed, then they walked along informal and untrodden woodland paths. On return the clearing was still empty; few people knew of its existence. Later they stopped off at a rural pub which offered meals other than the traditional Sunday roast. Hilary insisted on paying. Charles protested but she stood her ground. "Relationships cannot thrive without equality, so I will pay! Charles, I don't know the way forward, with each other… in this relationship, but we cannot go back now, can we?"

"I just need a little time to plan the best way to end my marriage. Please be patient with me… I love you, Hilary. Being together as we have today has given me a happiness I never dreamt of. I am only sorry that the practical arrangements are rather deceitful."

Hilary heard the word 'love' and felt it to be true. She galvanised herself to respond. "I don't think I have loved anyone in this way, Charles. It's difficult to explain, but I can't ignore it, or you, or the changes that need to take place."

"Changes? Apart from the end of my marriage?"

"We need a safe place for our love to either grow or wither. That doesn't really sound how I mean it to, but I am not yet sure whether you are an annual, a perennial or a shrub."

Charles was smiling. "I love your pragmatism! Only you can speak such words with tenderness. We will find a way—"

"I know the way." Hilary was forthright. "I was ready to tell Thistle to leave, and now that must happen."

"But can you cope financially without her? I could help out—"

"It is over eighteen months since I bought the maisonette, and of late my budget is under control. I don't need her rent, plus I do not need her to devour any more of my life."

"What do you mean?"

"Sadly, in addition to her other unsavoury personality traits, she is not to be trusted. For example, I wouldn't confess to her that you are married. If we are to continue then she might guess, and I dread to think where that may lead. Thistle is intensely possessive; she would do anything to cause a rift between us. I am finding her quite unnerving nowadays."

"Her graciousness was all an act earlier?"

"I have begun to think that Thistle may benefit from talking to a professional. Most of her life had been worse than vile when we became friends. I thought I could make a difference and it hurts me that I cannot, but her behaviour is becoming more erratic. She has to go."

Thistle was in bed, albeit awake, when Hilary arrived home. It was late. Hilary went straight into the bathroom. Monday heralded in June; it was one week before Hilary's twenty-sixth birthday. Having worked on Saturday she had an early finish and was pottering in the garden when Thistle returned from work. Hilary followed her into the kitchen.

"Tell me, Thistle – what was that little performance for Charles about yesterday? Did you think he would swallow your bait?"

"He would have, and he will, if you don't get in the way. Hilary, I am doing you a favour. I can demonstrate how fickle he is and then I will have saved you from being hurt."

"This is one of those uncommon occasions in which you have miscalculated your plan of action. The nature of Charles and my relationship is one that you cannot rupture, and I do not intend on enabling the opportunity for you to try. I have made the decision that it is time you sought alternative lodgings. I will give you to the end of June, but quite frankly I would prefer you to leave as soon as possible."

Feeling loved had provided Hilary with a hitherto rarely seen courage. Thistle, stunned for the second day running, saw the needle approach: a lethal injection. The end of her world.

"No, Hilary. You cannot injure me like this. I will die. I'm sorry. I know I have been a bit ratty lately, but I'll make more effort. I didn't mean those things I said. I was desperate. I didn't want to lose you. You must know that? I told you before – I would never do anything to harm you. You are my world, my rock. I love you." Thistle was shaking, but Hilary withstood an urge to console her.

"Thistle, I am not sure that you have the wherewithal to love anybody. I am saddened about that, but I have accepted reality and now I know that I, without hesitation, do not love you and probably never have."

Thistle's mask of repentance started to crumble as she began her lament. "All of this… all of what you say is just because I am female, isn't it? You can't allow yourself to love a woman. You're scared of judgement and discrimination. For Jesus Christ's sake – we are in the twentieth century. No-one turns a hair anymore. Don't be shackled by a few people's ignorance and intolerance. Strike out. Be brave. I will always be at your side—"

"*Enough.*" Hilary could hear mania emanating from Thistle's misguided lecture. "It has nothing to do with you being female! It is because of who you are as a person. Gender does not decree character. I once believed that through the continuity of our connection you could heal from the wounds that have scarred your life. I wondered whether a future with you might not be out of the question. I was confused for a while, but certainty gradually materialised. I might still be unsure about exactly what I want from life, but I have no doubts at all as to what I do *not* want. And I do not want this – *you*, here or anywhere."

"You don't understand. I have no-one, I…" Thistle had run out of steam. She recognised that pleading was futile.

"Take a look around and maybe you will understand why you have no-one. Yes, you are not responsible for being assaulted, abandoned and re-cycled from one situation to another like a cast-off sweater found in a jumble sale. But now I must speculate on whether the malice you so easily access has been within you, part of you, all along. You said that your parents used to argue, and the fact that they dismissed your life without pity suggests that one or both were capable of wickedness. Nature or nurture? In your case I hazard a guess at both. Please seek help from people who can get to the bottom of your problems – who know how you can mend – because I am backing off."

Thistle slammed out of the maisonette and sped off on her moped. "I know what I help I need," she told the tarmac road ahead. Shortly after six o'clock she walked into Bistead doctor's surgery and requested an emergency appointment. She was in luck. Thirty minutes later she was waiting at a local evening pharmacy for the processing of a prescription for tranquilisers, which were handed out like wine gums to anyone suffering from a relationship breakup.

The pharmacist let her have a glass of water to take her first dose with. Next stop was a phone box.

"Don? It's Thistle. I am in a bit of a fix. That woman I lodge with seems to be having a mental breakdown and I urgently need to find alternative accommodation. With all your contacts I hoped you might know of a vacant flat or bed-sit."

"Are you safe to stay there tonight, Thistle?"

"Oh yes – I don't think she is dangerous but definitely loony. It's horrible. The sooner I can get out, the better."

"I will ring around. If you do feel unsafe, we can put you up for a few days."

"Thank you, Don. You are too kind."

Ever since she had put Don on edge about sexual innuendo from the operatives, he had felt a sense of obligation towards her. As she left the phone box her words to Don repeated over and over in her head. In recent months there had been moments when Thistle was just waiting in the wings of her theatre of delusion; now she trooped out into her own spotlight. Hilary was having a breakdown. If Thistle moved out, Hilary would get better, miss her and ask Thistle to return. It was imperative that she get away for that process to begin. She and Hilary successfully dodged each other that evening; Thistle cuddled up to a whisky bottle whilst Hilary buried her head in a book.

In 1981 city suburbs were urban villages. Close-knit communities where favours were the oil that kept social machinery running smoothly. Don was owed plenty of handshakes. A furnished third-floor, one-bedroom flat on the northern flank of Bistead was available for cheap, cash rent because since the last legitimate tenant left, the owner was using it as a fraudulent false address.

"Probably tax avoidance. Don't ask questions," advised Don. All Thistle had to do was to be at the flat at six-thirty every Thursday for a courier to pick up the post, and she was not to draw attention to herself with neighbours. Don gave her the keys on Wednesday. On Thursday she took the day off to tour second-hand shops for additional kitchen and household equipment. She also visited a key cutter. That afternoon she gave the flat a thorough clean. It was in a 1960s block, a divided design of rendering and rust-coloured bricks. The third floor was also the top floor. The rooms, all painted dove-grey, weren't excessively big. A small balcony encased with black wrought-iron railings was accessed from lounge-diner glass doors. Across it she tied a washing line. The view looked directly over a similar building. At least she had her own bathroom which contained an undersized bath, no window, but instead an extractor fan. *I won't be here for long.* She was convinced of that. Mick offered her an old television set; hers had died not long before she moved in with Hilary. He brought it round after he finished work.

"Thistle," Mick said, "do you want me to move your things here in the van tomorrow? Save you lots of moped journeys. I can check out with Don for us to finish work early."

The next day they collected her belongings from the maisonette before Hilary returned from the library. Thistle was grateful but did not grasp that Mick's generosity was fuelled by hidden longing. To her he was a grimy, gruff, middle-aged loser. There was little time to unpack before she had to race off to the Duke. Mick was dismissed with a perfunctory 'thank you', then Panda was rested against the pillow of another single bed.

Hilary was staggered by Thistle's competency in finding a new home so quickly. She was also relieved that Thistle remained calm about it. Thistle's medication was keeping her emotions numbed and her conviction that it would be a temporary relocation kept her mind at peace. The two managed to avoid each other. After work on Tuesday Thistle visited Ruth and pretended to be interested in the baby. She gave no details about why she was having to 'temporarily' leave Hilary's. Wednesday saw Hilary take a bus straight from work to her parents' house on the pretence of checking it over. On Thursday, after cleaning the flat, Thistle waited for the courier to arrive, then she fiddled with the aerial of Mick's tarnished television. When Hilary returned from work on Friday there was no trace of Thistle, just a note, a birthday card and the front-door key. The note left a telephone number (the owner had agreed to bill her for telephone usage) and a request that she continue to use Hilary's address for post because, as Thistle worded it: "I do not expect to be there long – it is a stop-gap." Apart from her mistaken belief that Hilary would beg her to come back, it was a condition of the rental that she did not use the property as her postal address.

Hilary had mixed feelings when she read the note. Initially she was overwhelmed with guilt; Thistle was behaving in such an adult way that Hilary feared she may have treated her unfairly. Yet, as Hilary wandered around her home, which was now sanctuary for no-one except herself for the first time since January 1980, the guilt gradually diminished. *My space, my castle – my freedom.* The phone rang; it was Charles arranging to visit on Saturday evening as he could not make it on her birthday, and afterwards he would be working away for a few days. *And that is how it will be for a while*, she admitted to herself as she entered the kitchen and shoved two sausages under the grill. Apart from twinges of conscience about Anna, she did not mind one iota. At this stage in her life a part-time love ticked her emotional box. A box marked 'employment' was also being ticked; the surge of inductions following a library service recruitment drive had tailed off; they would now occur sporadically. However 'the powers that be' were talking to her about undertaking some management training in September. Hilary was reclaiming her integrated self. On Saturday morning she couldn't resist opening, two days early, a birthday card which arrived with a French postmark. It was a beautiful painting of French lavender fields. Inside was blank except for Fliss's untidy scrawl:

> *"Happy birthday H. It has been depressing here since Claude died but Didier is getting a manager. I will write when I know more. I just hope this new guy won't interfere with Le Pommier! Thinking of you. Hope all is well. Love F x"*

Hilary walked to Ashbrook shops, selected a photo-card of Lady Sarah's Park rhododendrons, and wrote it at a counter in the post office:

*"Hi F. Thanks for picturesque card. Thistle gone. I'm having an affair with a married man. That's what you call 'a nutshell'. Love H x"*

On Saturday evening after finishing her stint at the Anchor Inn, Thistle took the route which passed the maisonette. Charles's car was in the driveway. Then she stopped at the estuary. A cruise liner decked with garlands of fairy lights was in port. There seemed to be a party on board; she could almost hear the chime of piano keys. It was on this Saturday one year beforehand that Hilary and Fliss had entered the pub to celebrate Hilary's twenty-fifth birthday. Thistle remembered the occasion well. Now Charles was in situ. "It won't last," she confidently enlightened the ornamented ship.

Whilst Hilary was thrashing her way through brambles of identity to eventually surface as Charles's lover, Fliss was labouring under a mantle of mourning. The local community grieved Claude's death. "Last of his generation," they pined. Didier's wife and two eldest daughters were bereft, but none felt Claude's loss more acutely than his only son. Didier's erstwhile industriousness slithered like rainwater down a drain of inertia. Only Francine remained relatively untouched by it all, mainly because she was being regularly 'touched' by a farm labourer, usually in the third orchard along a track leading to the machinery storage barns. Fliss had hoped that the Easter break would leave the family feeling refreshed and renewed, but by her twenty-sixth birthday on April 25th nothing had changed, and Didier's conduct was becoming progressively abstract. She celebrated her birthday by drinking wine and calvados with Francine. It was a mild spring evening, so they took two chairs and a small table out into Fliss's imagined al fresco dining area. After the alcohol had succeeded in its purpose to liberate honesty, Fliss banged her glass down onto the table.

"I cannot stand it anymore, Francine. I know your grandpapa's passing is very sad, but life must go on. I must go on – with my dreams. Before we know it summer will have ended and there will have been nothing in this courtyard to accommodate townspeople or tourists. We should be opening up on weekend evenings again soon; I know we will get the custom."

Francine poured herself a calvados and nibbled on quiche left over from the lunchtime sitting.

Fliss continued, "I hate to say it, but your papa is not coping and that will impact on all of his business, not just my tiny venture. I never thought I would say this, but I think he does need to employ a manager. Francine, talk with your mama. Persuade her to rekindle the idea in Didier; he was thinking about it in March, but now he's apathetic about everything."

Didier's wife was sufficiently worried about him to carry out Fliss's suggestion. By late May a manager had been sourced. Didier appeared outside Le Pommier early one morning as Fliss was dragging tables and chairs out into the courtyard for morning coffee regulars. The sun was shining but not fiercely enough for people to need shade.

"Fliss – please welcome Mathieu. Mathieu – my cousin's daughter, Felice."

Following that brief introduction Didier absented himself. He knew that Fliss had been against the installation of a manager. He did not know that it was her who had driven the idea forward. Believing that she was likely to give Mathieu short shrift, he quit the scene.

"Good morning," said Mathieu with a polished English accent. Fliss was stumped for words. He not only spoke English, but he also looked English. Tall, broad-shouldered; she also noticed his broad forehead, broad cheekbones, broad chin and currently a broad grin.

A mischievous thought caused her to titter, *I think I will name you Norfolk… because you are full of broads.* Mathieu was still grinning, but his attention seemed to be over her shoulder. "Is there something wrong?" she asked.

"A brown stain… it's running down your right cheek…"

Her forefinger wiped the cheek; she studied it. "Chocolate. I have been baking individual chocolate tortes to accompany morning coffee." She licked the finger and dried it on her apron. "You speak English like an Englishman. Didier told us all you are French."

"Half and half. Long story. So – do you need help with those tables?"

"No. I can manage." Fliss was assertively establishing her dominance of Le Pommier.

"I gather you would like to create a proper al fresco area. And at some time convert a barn into a restaurant and spare land into a campsite. Big plans."

"How can someone achieve big things if they don't think '*big*' in the first place?"

Mathieu was aware that there were bristles forming along Fliss's spine. She was too but could not determine the reason. He decided on tactfulness. "When I have settled into the position perhaps I can try your patisseries and you can elucidate. Nice to have met you, Felice."

"Fliss – I respond to the name Fliss."

"Mat – but I also respond to 'hey you'!" He grinned once more and left.

"Well, don't take too long settling in, 'Mat', because I need my al fresco area," burbled Fliss as she walked back to the kitchen, pulling at the dotty headscarf that still hid her sleek black hair.

Francine arrived. "What's he like?"

Fliss answered, "He is like Norfolk."

"What's Norfolk?"

Fliss, bristles still in place: "It is a place full of broads."

"I thought broads were the women in Hollywood movies—"

"Oh, never mind, Francine. Perhaps I will nickname him door-Mat – because that is what I need right now!" They laughed, although Francine wasn't sure why, but Fliss's comments always made her giggle.

It was a Wednesday, late afternoon in mid-June. Fliss had glimpsed Mathieu flitting around the farm, but he had not returned to discuss her proposals, and this infuriated her. She was fed up with continually moving tables and chairs in and out depending on the sun, the heat, occasional rain or strong breezes. *I might as well be a bloody weathervane.* A pile of post had arrived. She picked it up along with a bottle of beer and headed for the nearest orchard. When she was young the family visited Grandmamma every summer and this refuge of trees was the place she ran to after throwing tantrums. Often she would fall asleep in the dappled shade and dream of nymphs and fairies. Now she was dreaming of punching an English form of Frenchman on the nose. *They're all the same – men. I am much better off now I don't give a damn about them.* Swigging her beer, Fliss flicked through the letters and noticed Hilary's card. She nearly choked as she repeatedly read Hilary's few words. "This isn't a nutshell, Hilary – it's a mighty bombshell!" Lighting a Gauloises, she leaned her back against a tree, blew smoke rings into the air, closed her eyes and gurgled with bliss, like a baby with its comfort blanket. *I do hope that this is Hilary's missing bouquet...* A cough intruded into her cheerful moment. She opened her eyes and her mouth drooped.

"Francine told me you weren't very happy, but you looked as pleased as punch a moment ago. She said I would find you here... Fliss. May I join you?" Mathieu was presenting like a dog with its tail between its legs.

"Of course... Mat." Fliss offered him a Gauloises, but he pulled a packet of Dunhill out of his pocket.

"I prefer English cigarettes."

"And why would a Frenchman prefer an English brand?" Fliss copied the tone of voice from a remembrance of her very first infant-school teacher, who effectively blackmailed a canny, deliberately mute Fliss into talking to people, on the threat that the school would call her 'Felice' if she did not. It seemed a lifetime ago, but the memory of that formidable woman had never dimmed.

"Long story."

"Well – go on. You can't keep saying 'long story'. What is it… *Lord of the Rings*?" (Fliss had never read *Lord of the Rings*, but Hilary had.)

Mat looked towards a natural dell amongst the apple trees. Rays of sunshine danced like ballerinas and invited passing shadows to prance within their ballet. The setting was ambient even if the young woman sat beside him was a bush of unyielding holly.

"It was like this…" Taking twenty words to describe each event where just a few would have been adequate, he explained his story. Something about his delivery was familiar to Fliss. *Who else jabbers on and on like this?* she pondered. The content of his saga was in some ways coincidentally similar to her own, but a generation apart. His father had been an English medic on French soil during World War Two. He met and married a French nurse. They returned to live in Sussex, where he trained as a GP. Mat had an older brother who had followed his father into the medical profession. His mother had died of cancer a few years ago. Like Fliss's family, his had also visited French relations over the years.

Eventually Fliss found the gap to ask a question: "So you grew up in England but now you are working here?"

"I trained as a company accountant and found well-paid employment. I learned quite a bit about commerce and industry but… accountancy is boring, so boring… I could go on…"

"No, don't bother, I get the picture."

"Relatives with a farm on the southern edge of Calais have a dairy herd. They decided on a new enterprise – an ice-cream factory using milk from their cows. They had the technical knowledge but knew nothing about the business side. I was missing my recently deceased mother and needed to escape the drudge of England so offered them my services for board and lodging. That was nearly two years ago, and the business is doing well. They make the most delicious ice-cream cakes! Somehow they know Didier."

"Through livestock, I guess."

"Yes, probably. I needed to add strings to my bow; working here is a golden opportunity even though I know it's only temporary – until he finds his feet again."

"That could take longer than you think!"

"What about you? You are patently English despite the name to which you don't answer."

"I am a quarter French."

"Beat you then, as I am half!"

"Touché." Fliss couldn't help herself – her lips curled into that famous smirk. She thought about Hilary's card: 'a nutshell'; and experimenting with a previously untried gambit, Fliss gave a summary account of her French alliance and association in exactly that: a nutshell. "So that's it, Mat – now you know why I am here."

"Look, Fliss – I came to apologise. I meant to get back to you about the al fresco area, and I have noticed you lugging furniture in and out."

Her prickles had softened during their story-sharing. "It's alright. I realise you must be tied up trying to unravel the mess Didier was making of everything." She picked up her post and the empty bottle, ready to leave.

"Fliss, do you know of anywhere nearby that sells heavy-duty garden furniture, parasols and pots?"

"Yes, a hyper-market garden centre on a retail estate on the outskirts of Le Havre – if they still have stock."

"What are you doing on Sunday? Church?"

"No way."

"I will release some funds from the business account, borrow a trailer and you can show me where it is. We will buy what we can for now and I will set it up."

"But Sunday is your only day off."

"My boarding house in the town isn't very thrilling. Once I have washed my 'smalls' I will be free." Mat was grinning again.

*Grinning man, that's my nickname for you, not Norfolk or door-Mat*, Fliss silently decided.

"I couldn't possibly allow you to do that on your day off."

"Of course you can; you need that outdoor space – and soon. I will think of it as a working day and determine a way that you can make recompense – free patisseries for the remainder of my stay, maybe?"

"Thank you," she said, modestly.

Fliss was experiencing a brand-new feeling: coyness. She noticed her chipped fingernails which had not been manicured for nine months. She used one to scratch at her chin; there was no liquid foundation to be trapped underneath it. Her unenhanced eyes were drawn to her well-worn jeans that bore the spilt remains of today's cooking.

Her hand reached up to the cotton headscarf; wisps of hair were escaping it in an untidy fashion. *Good job I don't fancy grinning man*, she told herself.

On Sunday Fliss awoke with the cockerel. She decided that her hair could do with a wash and condition. Once that was completed, she rifled through her vanity case and found a claw-clip hair accessory. She wound her locks up into a bun, sealed the ball with a hairband and fastened the clip over the top. Then she tipped out her makeup bag; the liquid foundation had congealed but eyeshadow and mascara had survived months of idleness. The decision of what to wear took so long that she had to skip breakfast. All the time she was totally unaware of her change in behaviour. Mat arrived and hid a smile as she stepped out into the courtyard.

*She's made an effort. Maybe she does like me after all*, he thought, with hope. His beaten-up wreck of an estate car had a towbar; the trailer bounced behind them on the journey. He remarked on the countryside; she pointed out notable places. Together they loaded flat-packed tables that would need construction, matching patio chairs, robust floor-standing parasols and a selection of gaily painted pots. There was no room left for the plants to fill them, but Fliss said she could pick some up during the week from Pont l'Eveque's nursery. Back at Le Pommier she prepared omelettes whilst Mat began erecting the tables. After lunch he continued. It was a steamy day and torrents of sweat formed lakes around stubble that he had allowed to form on his broad chin. *Yes – stubble definitely produces a classic film-star face.* That had been his opinion when he preened himself in front of the bathroom mirror that morning. He would never have a film star's face, but the fact that on this day he wanted one so badly, verified a force of magnetism which was pulling him towards the petite yet feisty female to whom he had given the nickname 'Chocolate Éclair': an artificially hardened exterior disguising a yummy, mushy, indulgent centre. Fliss ran a cool iron over large, checked all-weather tablecloths that she had bought months beforehand in readiness for the courtyard transformation. Together they arranged the purchases and her image of Le Pommier's al fresco area began to take shape.

"Fliss – if you pick up some trellis I will put it up after work one day this week."

She handed him a beer which he downed in one swallow. She immediately offered him another and they sat to evaluate their efforts.

"It looks great, thank you so much, Mat."

"Add your divine inspiration and you will have created a work of art. I noticed the Picasso poster on the wall inside. You have good taste."

"My friend gave it to me for my twenty-fifth birthday." An apparition of Hilary appeared, which only Fliss could see.

*Thank goodness you are here, Hilary – help me. What do I do? What do I say?* The invisible Hilary, who was merely a product of Fliss's fancy, whispered sound advice in her ear. "Get to know him. Treat him like a friend and there's a chance that the buds of your bonding may blossom into love." In time Fliss would learn that it was her own inner voice counselling on next steps. For now, she heeded the first suggestion. The remnants of femme fatale and disco diva were thrown into a slurry pit. With purposeful civility she asked, "Tell me, Mat – what might you usually be doing on a Sunday? What is your favourite hobby?"

"Fly-fishing." His face was deadpan, no hint of a grin.

"How... fascinating," lied Fliss, wishing that she knew how to convey enthusiasm. Suddenly the deadpan face erupted into a volcano of laughter. "Sorry – I was joking!"

Fliss did not know whether to join him in hilarity or cry into her beer. She was making so much effort to be polite and take a genuine interest. She was speechless. The real Hilary would have been dumbfounded by Fliss's lack of instant wit.

"I am sorry, Fliss. I can be naughty at times." Mat raised his brows and pinched his mouth into a pout of regret. He held out the palm of his hand as he often used to do for a schoolteacher who was fond of using the cane, which Mat recurrently received. She smacked it with a rolled-up serviette. Fliss's own grin was breaking through her conjecture that she was the director of male-focussed proceedings, not the man.

"Actually, cycling is my top hobby, but I also enjoy Boules; lots of evidence of my French blood! What about you?"

"I am improving my written French, but I don't believe I have ever had a hobby, though cooking was, until I turned it into work." She did not think that boozing and hip-swinging counted as pastimes. Fliss remembered Hilary's admonition: *Find a hobby.*

"What are you up to next Sunday? You know the area, I don't. If you are free, I would like to be shown around. I have my bike here – we could cycle."

"Mat, I don't have a bicycle."

"Francine does. I have seen her use it to tour the orchards."

Fliss bit her lip. *Tour? No, I had better not tell him about her true interest in orchards.*

Mat was still talking: "I am sure she would loan it to you." He was grinning again. Even his eyes were smiley. His disposition gleamed like rays of sun cavorting through the apple trees: merry, warm and reassuring. His broad shoulders would carry the weight of the world.

Fliss took the plunge: "After all your hard work today the least I can do is cook you an evening meal."

"That would be fantastic. Thank you, Fliss. But I am now rather filthy and extremely smelly, so do you mind if I pop back to my lodgings for a shower and change?"

Mind? How could she mind? He would return, squeaky clean, with the aroma of Romeo. Her wish was for the buds to blossom, but she knew that they would only flower if she treated the tree with care, consideration and respect.

The following Friday evening Fliss watched the clock for the hour that she knew Hilary would be home from work and have eaten. She called the number. Hilary's voice: "Hello…" sounded like manna from heaven.

"Hilary – I think we have far too much gossip for letters! Have you got time for a natter? Your card arrived… I have so much to ask you about and just a wee amount to pass on – nutshells not coconut shells!"

"But ringing is so expensive for you."

"It's worth every penny to hear your dulcet tones!"

"Ha, ha. So – who is going first?"

"*You* – come on, spill the beans!"

# 10

# Last-Chance
# Saloon

ON THE SUNDAY of Thistle's first weekend in 'bleak house', as she had named the block of flats, she decided on a lengthy walk to familiarise herself with the area, which she discovered was listed as 'Bistead Manor' after a now-demolished manor house. That explained the address of the flats: Manor Close. It became clear that until the end of the 1960s this northern neighbourhood of Bistead had marked an outer-city boundary; it had drawn a definitive line between suburbia and agricultural countryside. As the 1970s progressed so increasing swathes of farmland and hamlets were swallowed up by urban development. The scale of destruction formed a picture in Thistle's mind as she discovered yet more felled trees, ripped hedgerows and construction machinery lying in wait to churn up the soil and smother it with concrete and bitumen. She asked a passing dog-walker, "What's going on over there?" and pointed towards an expansive chasm coursing its way through rolling hillsides.

"A new motorway to by-pass the entire city, including this next housing development you see in front of you. The properties are being thrown up as quickly as Lego models but without the same level of skill." The dog-walker's age was hard to determine but he was old enough to know Bistead Manor's history. He wiped a tear from his eye.

"You have seen a lot of change?" she asked with, unusually for her, compassion and sympathy.

"Oh yes, and none of it good. As a lad I used to run through the wheat fields and help at strawberry-picking time. Me and my mates cycled the lanes without seeing a car. We roamed from dawn to dusk, and the only noise was birdsong and animal calls. Progress, they call this. Ugly and brutal. World War Two bombardments didn't destroy nature on this scale, but post-war men have detonated a bomb of colossal catastrophe. Where will it all end? Eh?" He shuffled along the road with an ageing terrier who was just able to keep up the pace.

Thistle spun around to begin her return journey, noticing the road names: 'Clover Way', 'Buttercup Close', 'Strawberry Fields'. "The next road should be named 'Ironic'," she said aloud to deserted streets. Most homes were already lived in but on this Sunday afternoon there was little sign of life. After a while she came across The Wheatsheaf, an 'olde world', country-style pub which was the remaining building from a once-remote hamlet, now finding itself embedded within a sprawl of commuter belt.

*That's strange – I don't remember passing this*, she thought. Then it dawned on her: she was lost. A maze of cul-de-sacs and crescents linked by interconnecting footways and estate side roads surrounded her. She walked up to the pub's front door; The Wheatsheaf did not open until six o'clock. It was now five thirty-five. A woman walked past to collect her children from a neighbour's garden. When asked if she knew where Manor Close was, she shook her head and scurried by. Thistle did not intend on waiting in the hope that the publican would know the location of Manor Close so took the road that she thought was most likely to provide an escape route from this clumsily assembled rabbit warren. After ten minutes she could see slightly older-style houses in the distance and the rugby-ball figure of a man walking towards her carrying a large sackcloth bag. "George," she shouted as he came clearly into view; it was 'old George' – wallpaperer extraordinaire.

"What the flip are you doing here, missus?"

"I'm lost! I moved into a flat in Manor Close on Friday and cannot find my way back. Is it this way? Do you know it?"

"Oh yes – it's me picking you up in the morning. You and I have a job on all this week at a posh house out east. Don called to tell me where you were, but…" He scratched his head.

"But what?"

"Well – you are walking in the wrong direction. I would show you how to get there but I have to drop off these spuds from my garden to the wife's brother, then I am meeting Mick in The Wheatsheaf for a bevvy or two."

Thistle conjured up her best impression of a forlorn fawn.

George felt guilty. "Look – I will walk you to a road from where you should be able to find your way back. I'm sure Mick will understand when I explain why I am late. Anyway – he can get the first pints in." George chuckled.

"Does Mick live near there then?" Thistle couldn't imagine that Mick would live on a modern estate; he did not seem the type.

George nodded. "Funny how life turns out for some people. Come on, this way."

A link road provided Thistle with her route to Manor Close, which was not too far from The Wheatsheaf as the crow flies, but knowledge of the footways was vital. The endless labyrinth of homes for humanity made her wonder about the far-west perimeter of the city, where she had lived with Eric and Vida. She made up her mind to scooter over there the following weekend. The next day brought work, and it was Hilary's birthday. She hoped Hilary liked the card, which had a picture of interlocked teddies on the front. Inside Thistle had written: "Love from your forever friend." Enclosed in it was a pin brooch: an owl design, wrapped in a small piece of tissue paper. That evening Hilary did not ring to thank Thistle. Thistle picked up the phone to ring her, paused and put it down. Then she poured a glass of whisky with which to wash down two tranquilisers.

By Thursday evening Thistle could no longer hold back. She phoned on the pretext that she was enquiring whether there had been any post. Hilary used the minimum number of words to express gratitude for the gift and told her what looked like a bank statement had arrived that day. Thistle said she could collect it on Saturday en route to the Anchor Inn. Hilary said she would not be at home but could leave it under the door mat. She did not ask how Thistle was. On Saturday evening Thistle collected the letter; there was no sound from the maisonette. She peered through a couple of windows, but Hilary could not be seen. After her pub session she scootered back. There was no car outside, but a dim light was scantily apparent from Hilary's bedroom window. She wanted to knock on the door. The green-eyed devil was burning inside; where had Hilary been? Thistle had to know. A police car was parked further down the street. Thistle moved on, without learning the truth: Charles had not been available on Saturday. Hilary had visited Sandra and stayed for lunch, which her husband prepared as the baby was central to Sandra's every move. It felt uplifting to have that old friend back in her life. She had caught the early evening bus back to Ashbrook.

Thistle's plan to travel west of the city on Sunday had to be postponed; recent balmy temperatures triggered thunderstorms which arrived first thing and did not subside. Her transistor radio was producing a tinny, scratchy sound. *I need a radio-cassette player*, she decided. Hilary had introduced Thistle to classical music and now she had several cassette tapes, in addition to a tape collection of easy listening songs, but nothing to play them on. *I miss Hilary's radio-cassette. I miss the garden and walking by the estuary. Most of all I miss having a piano to play.* Thistle was jealous of whom Hilary might be with and incensed that she had no control over her life, but when it came to a list of what she missed, Hilary's name was not forefront in her mind.

The job at the 'posh' house was a long one; Thistle was with 'old George' for a second week. She did not mind George. He was the only remaining one of 'old boy operatives' who were working for Don when she had started. George bumbled along, passing on-going comments about the state of the world, Thatcher's policies and the damage that woodpigeons were doing to his vegetable plot. Thistle rarely listened. On their way to work one day, looking to change the subject from the upcoming royal wedding, she chipped in, "How come Mick lives on that hodgepodge housing estate?"

Like so many men who berate their wives for gossiping, George immensely enjoyed an opportunity for rumour and scandal. "His wife left him some years ago. He didn't do too well from the divorce settlement. Bought a flat, but by end of last year he had saved enough for a new build, three-bed semi-detached."

"He can have his kids stay then?"

"No kids – that was the problem. That's why she flew the coop. It seems he could cut the mustard but had no cream in his custard." He winked. "Get the drift?"

Thistle did not like to admit that she didn't, but later in the day whilst dipping a paintbrush into paint, the penny dropped. She imagined all the operatives having a good laugh about Mick's lack of fertility. *Men are so insensitive*, said the queen of hearts.

On Saturday, full of apprehension, Thistle crossed to the west of the city. Her worst fears were confirmed as she arrived at the lane leading to Eric and Vida's 'Hansel and Gretel' house. The once single-track road had been widened into a two-lane carriageway. It enabled access to a reproduction of Bistead Manor. *No fields, no trees; no birds, no bees,* she sang in her head. Scootering along the new road she reached the house. Outside was a large board announcing 'Luxury flats for sale or rent'. The gingerbread house had been converted. *Eric must have sold it – I wonder where he is. Vida will be turning in her grave.* Most of the front garden had been tarmacked to provide parking. Tiptoeing around the side she was confronted by a row of garages and space for rubbish bins in what little remained of the formal gardens. Only a couple of oaks were still standing, grateful for their amnesty as they presided over the ragged remains of a shrub border. A voice called out, "Oy, what you doing here? Off you go – you're trespassing. Go on – sod off." Thistle needed no encouragement to leave; she had seen enough. Her eyes were smarting with tears. *A radio-cassette player... that's what I need... to cheer myself up.*

She headed for the city centre, to Williams and Brown department store. The ground floor housed the electrical department. She was browsing merchandise when the rear of an auburn head caught her eye. He was with a woman who resembled Hilary: same height, colouring and build, except this woman was not wearing spectacles and her hair was scraped back into a ponytail. They were studying televisions. *Jesus, Charles is cheating on Hilary with another woman,* thought Thistle. She kept her distance and watched. Making no purchase they headed towards the escalator. In a trice Thistle was at the bottom of the stairs to the upper floors. She ran up the steps with the agility of a cheetah, having no idea as to which floor they were heading. On the next floor was Fliss's ladies' fashions, now signed as 'W&B's Boutique'. Thistle guessed this floor to be a good bet. Carefully side-stepping between rails of ladies clothing, she spotted Charles and the woman, who was holding up a jade-green party dress as he looked on admiringly. Something was glinting in the glare of light bulbs; shiny chinks on the third finger of the woman's left hand. Thistle saw the truth: *He's married. I must tell Hilary. She will be shocked, upset – but she will come around and then we can continue as before.*

Thistle returned to the flat to change clothes, but there was no time to expose Charles's other life to Hilary before she started at the Anchor Inn. Once again, after playing piano and collecting a few pounds, she scootered the short distance to Hilary's maisonette. Charles's car was outside. *How can he?* In addition to her latest sub-personality – Queen of Hearts – Thistle was also playing 'Princess of Propriety'. She had to bide her time until Hilary returned from her parents' house on Sunday afternoon. Thistle had walked the estuary, practising her script. Hilary did not appear pleased to see Thistle but invited her in. "There is no more post for you."

"Hilary, I am so sorry to be bearer of bad news. Whatever I have done in the past I am also sorry for. You don't deserve anything other than loyalty."

Hilary did not appreciate grovelling. "Out with it. What do you really want to say?"

"I was shopping yesterday when I saw Charles. Hilary, he has been lying to you – he is married." Thistle was armed with a toolbox of appropriate responses to the shock, horror and distress this announcement was going to cause. Except, those did not happen. Hilary's eyes remained focussed and unperturbed. Her body did not even quiver.

"Jesus – you know!" exclaimed Thistle, who was the one filled with shock and horror. "How can you be so immoral – with your upbringing?"

Hilary did not voice her answer. *Maybe it is precisely because of being contained, tethered and emotionally squashed for so much of my life I needed to lift the lid, break chains and set free the secrets of Pandora's Box.* Instead, she replied, "And what do you intend to do with your discovery, Thistle? It had better be 'nothing', because it is absolutely none of your business, but please be aware that he is planning to leave his wife and their unhappy, unfulfilling marriage."

"Well, they looked amazingly happy and fulfilled to me. I think you are fooling yourself. Get a grip, Hilary. See the truth. Men are always going to leave their wives – but they never do. Unless you finish it now, you will be dangling on the end of his string as well as his dick until he tires of you."

Hilary had given Thistle enough string, and she had hung herself with those final words. Hilary responded with a tone of confined thunder: "*Go*, just *go*. Please depart before I say something about you that is better left unsaid. And arrange for your post to go elsewhere. From now on I will be returning everything to sender. Don't you *ever* come here again."

On Saturday evening Charles had informed Hilary that Anna's mother was very unwell; it was probably asbestosis.

He would have to wait until Anna was mentally strong again before proposing a divorce. Anna's mother was ailing; this was no lie. Charles did want to leave Anna and maybe he would. Eventually every 'maybe' results in a decision that can drive its maker into a personal heaven or hell. Outcomes are the rewards or penalties for choices made.

Thistle had choices. She could turn a page and look forward to the next chapter.

However, she was not sure what had happened in the previous and felt compelled to re-write it in words that she could comprehend. The lid of her own Pandora's Box had been blasted to smithereens. She lay on her lonely bed, mesmerised by all manner of demons and fiends zooming around above her head. "*Sento la ninna nanna del diavolo.*" She crooned these few lines from an Italian song popularised in the 1950s: 'I hear the Devil's lullaby'. Thistle had not undressed. At 11pm she put three items in a bag: a penknife, a small torch and Panda. Then she scootered back to the maisonette. Using the key she'd had cut before leaving, she soundlessly let herself in. Hilary's bedroom door creaked as Thistle opened it, but Hilary remained fast asleep. Thistle stealthily crept towards the bed, her hands outstretched. *It would be so easy*. A fork in the path, another choice: exorcise her grief, her hobgoblins and affliction. 'I must survive' – that mantra, the bedrock on which she stood. Any action could be justified in the name of survival. God would forgive. She would be given absolution. None of this was her fault; she would be exonerated. Hilary's body rolled onto its side. The movement interrupted Thistle's train of thought. Looking down at her hands, she saw white knuckles and sturdy, forceful fingers. Their purpose had always been to create something that people would love, from the flick of piano keys to the swish of a paintbrush. Could these same hands squeeze the breath out of another human being? Her fingers reached forward, curling slightly inwards, tempted to enfold their victim's neck. Then they unfurled. Taking the penknife and Panda from her bag, she slashed the tatty, cuddly toy across its tummy and pulled out some of the straw wadding. She left it on the end of Hilary's bed as a memento.

Hilary was awakened by her alarm clock and felt something resting on her feet: Panda, mutilated and disowned. *My God, Fliss was right. I could not see the darkness inside Thistle. I have always had faith that parts of her were in contrast, but like this Panda, perhaps even those areas have aged to grey. And... she has a key.*

Still disturbed by the knowledge of Thistle's presence in her bedroom, Hilary left early for work and looked up details for a locksmith. Then she phoned her parents, invented a story about a flooded bathroom and asked to stay for a couple of days. They obliged; there was a list of jobs waiting for her. The lock was changed on Thursday. That evening Charles phoned, concerned that she had not been answering her telephone. Hilary did not mention Thistle's nocturnal visit or that she knew Charles was married. She used the water leak excuse and made light about the change of door lock: "Just a precaution. I think Thistle may still have a key, and I wouldn't want her bursting in on us."

Hilary's feelings of guilt menaced her like a praying mantis: *What if I am to blame? Am I the root cause of her erraticism? I may have pushed her fragility too far.* One day Hilary would confide in Fliss. No-one else. But it was not the right time for this when she received Fliss's chirpy phone call.

Hilary was safe from Thistle. Thistle's attack on Panda had partly assuaged wrath born of rejection. With her penknife she had cut the ropes attaching her consciousness to the anchor of childhood. Panda had been murdered and left for someone else to bury. Mick picked her up on Monday morning. "S'truth – what's happened to you?" He couldn't help but notice her swollen, red eyes.

"I have to find a different postal address. I can't use that mad woman's place anymore. She's gone potty."

"Use mine. I'll write it down."

"Are you sure – won't anyone mind?" Thistle knew there was no-one to mind. "That is kind of you, Mick. Could you do me another favour?"

"Suppose," he said, with a voice of gravel.

"I have seen a radio-cassette player I want to buy in Williams and Brown. It is too big for me to carry on my moped. Could we pick it up in the van the next time we are near the city centre?"

"No problem. We can go over that way on Wednesday, I need the builder's merchants… we'll get it then." After a while he asked, "Are you settling into the flat alright?"

"I guess so – there are things I miss, especially the piano."

This week's 'job' was the painting of external rendering. Mick and Thistle worked quietly and attentively. As Mick dropped her off at 'Bleak House' he said, "George told me how you got lost down by The Wheatsheaf."

"Yes – sorry, I delayed him from meeting you."

"It is what you said this morning, about missing the piano. The Wheatsheaf has a piano. No-one plays it. At weekends customers want piped music but I reckon the landlord would let you play it on a weeknight – for fun. You already play at weekends, don't you?" Thistle wondered how Mick knew this, but she liked the idea of an extra tinkle. "Try it tomorrow," he continued, "because the guys play cribbage on Monday evenings."

"Thanks, Mick. Perhaps I will if I don't get lost."

"There is a quick way you can walk from here, right through the estate. I'll draw it for you. See you in the morning."

As Thistle climbed two flights of stairs to the flat, the part of her hooked on to surviving clocked Mick's interest.

She did not go to The Wheatsheaf on Tuesday evening. Mental exhaustion left her fit only for sleeping. Plus she expected that Hilary would phone. There had been no call on Monday evening; surely Hilary would want to have a rant. Any attention was better than no attention, but Hilary wasn't going to sit on that seesaw.

"I was knackered," Thistle explained to Mick on Wednesday morning, "So I didn't go. I'll go next Tuesday."

He said nothing. He knew she hadn't gone; he had propped up the bar all evening. In conversation with the landlord, Mick remarked on her piano-playing. "She plays for a couple of pubs at weekends. An uncle who uses the Duke of Wellington told me about a young pianist with ice-blonde hair and the bluest eyes. The description matched Thistle, so I popped over one Friday evening. It was her. She didn't see me, and I didn't stay long enough to be noticed, but I hung around for a while and realised that she's talented. Not your average sort of girl, in any way."

"What do you mean?"

"She's hard to fathom."

"Fancy her, do you?"

"No, mate – too young for me."

"How old are you anyway?"

"Thirty-seven."

The landlord had excellent customer service skills; he did not admit that he thought Mick to be much older – middle-aged.

❦

Thistle's mental health was walking a tightrope. She needed a safety net. After a weekend visit to Ruth, she recognised that the mother of a baby has her hands full. Thistle could no longer position herself as centre of Ruth's attention, but she felt the need to try. The upshot was that her language became uncouth and crude as she made defamatory remarks about the few real people in her life, and the many celebrity people spread over every newssheet. At one point Jed took the baby out of earshot; it could not have understood Thistle's insults, but Jed feared it would pick up on her negative energy. It was as if Thistle was clambering over the weaknesses she believed existed in others, in order to demonstrate an invincibility that was fast deserting her.

When Mick again encouraged her to play The Wheatsheaf's piano she agreed if he would meet her there. She supped a few whiskies for Dutch courage and, using his map, easily found the pub. This hostelry attracted a completely different clientele than the Duke and the Anchor. There were a few antique vestiges from The Wheatsheaf's bucolic past, who cast their eyes over Thistle and queried with each other as to why she was standing with 'the greasy Greek', but overall the customers were working men. The pub was their boys' club, a playground for egos to debate important issues of the world – football, cars and tabloid politics. At weekends for a treat, they would allow their wives into this secret society, ply them with sweetened liquor and pass around the school-boy 'nod' that was decoded as: *My luck's in tonight*. Because Thistle had worked with men for so long, she was not intimidated by this institution. After a couple more drinks (she could now handle her alcohol in-take as good as any man) she sat at the piano and realised there was no requirement to churn out old favourites. Indifferent to anyone's expectations, she played what she wanted to, and improvised as the mood took her, just as she used to at Hilary's. She played softly, not wishing to disturb the male fraternity. Mick moved to a chair near the piano. She was aware of his presence but ignored it. The landlord brought over another whisky for her. For an hour and a half Thistle was cast adrift from all that tormented her, and Mick was spell-bound. It was nearly closing time and Thistle had just left the ladies' toilet when a slick young man in his early thirties accosted her as she reached the lounge bar.

"A beauty who has talent… how about coming round for a night-cap and you can tell me all about—"

He did not complete his sentence. Mick nudged him out of the way, slipped his arm through Thistle's and escorted her out. He sent a clear message to any man who thought she was fair game: 'hands off'. Outside he offered to walk her home 'for safety'.

"There's no need for you to do that. I'm not scared."

"And I am not 'coming on' to you, Thistle."

"I know. You are a good man. Thank you."

Thistle needed to walk alone, to clear her head, to re-balance. The safety net had arrived. She never expected that its material would be made of maleness.

Tuesday evenings, playing with savvy spontaneity at The Wheatsheaf, helped Thistle pass the difficult weeks of July. This time of year had previously always lifted her mood: walking, gardening; saturating herself with summer. She bought two planted containers and put them on the balcony. She stopped scootering past the maisonette on Saturday evenings. Apart from playing at the Anchor Inn she avoided the area. No more sighting cruise liners on the estuary. No shared experiences. Little human interaction except for work and a repeat visit to the surgery for another prescription for tranquilisers.

Mick spoke with Don: "Where possible, can you rota her on with me or George?"

"Why?"

"I have a concern – that's all it is, boss."

Don was preoccupied with the fact that he would have to give the operatives the day off for the royal wedding. "Another public holiday. How is a man supposed to make profits?"

"The royal wedding is next Wednesday," said Mick to Thistle as they packed up the van one afternoon. "The Wheatsheaf is having a 'wedding party'."

"A what?"

"A wedding party! Lots of pubs are – to celebrate. Don has to give us the day off so that we can watch the procession on telly."

"Why does anyone want to watch rich people get hitched in all their finery, when so many ordinary people are out of work and struggling? It was only back in May that they were marching on London in protest."

Mick had no answer to this question; he continued, "Well, we are in work and a party will be fun. George and his missus are going. I have heard that women are planning to wear wedding dresses."

"Uugghh. How sick-making – pass me that bucket." Thistle pretended to put her fingers down her throat and brayed like a donkey.

"At least it has made you laugh."

She felt caught out, having resolved never to even smile again.

Thistle had annual leave owing to her but, having nowhere to go and no-one to go with, she had struck a deal with Don to be paid in lieu. Thus, a paid day off in the middle of the week felt a luxury. Against her better judgement she, along with the nation, watched the royal wedding. *Chastity united with pomposity*, was her opinion. In a few months' time her own marriage would be legally ended. With this thought she imagined herself as a gust of wind whistling though a tunnel – heading somewhere, destination… nowhere.

Mick phoned. "It is a glorious day, so – are you coming down the pub? There's a free buffet and a bloke with an accordion to jolly everyone up. It kicks off at six o'clock. Wedding dresses are not compulsory!"

Thistle had cut up the dress she married Ronnie in, for rags; the operatives never took enough of them out on jobs and as Thistle was always the one to clean up, she decided to supply her own. She sat on the balcony with a glass of wine; it made a change for a life so deficient in variety. Far below, in the grounds surrounding the blocks of flats, children played out being Prince Charles and Lady Diana. Adults had given them various garments to dress up in. Dressing-up clothes. Thistle felt queasy. She closed her eyes and, to hinder the onset of a memory, began to sing: "*Deep bubbles catch my breath, so content to be lonely. Teardrops are all I have left, – the smile that you see is phoney.*"

There was no way that she would 'dress up'. From a wardrobe hanger she yanked the cream gypsy skirt she had worn on the day that she first met Ronnie. A tight, sleeveless, laced-front, black tee-shirt was then pulled over her head. In an old handbag she found a ruby-red lipstick, which she applied to her normally pale lips. The effect was virtue matched with danger. She was inviting the world to its last chance: the chance not to give in to temptation, not to defile her body or pollute her lifeblood.

It was not just Mick and George who were hit for six when Thistle made her appearance; so too were a couple of the younger operatives who had decided to join the celebrations. No-one had seen her wear anything other than overalls, jeans and sweatshirts. In that garb and because of her leanness, her body could have been mistaken for being the young buck of a teenage boy. She approached them with a cynical twist of her contoured, blushing mouth to condescendingly tantalise. *Still think I'm a lesbo?* They read her mind.

Many men wore wedding suits or Union Jack sashes. Mick didn't. He was not the type to draw attention to himself. He could have easily blended into the background if it had not been for his jet-black hair. Mick had spent many years hiding in corners, usually pub corners. He had cut down on his smoking after advice from the doctor during a bout of pleurisy but ignored the same guidance regarding alcohol. On the evening of the royal wedding, he paced himself, not wanting to lose control. He had two reasons: firstly he wanted to be Thistle's bodyguard, ensure he kept her from the hedonistic debauchery which could result from a man being intoxicated by a mixture of drink and desire. The second reason was to keep her from exactly the same in himself. Since his wife left he had visited the city's red-light district a few times, but it had not met his needs.

Thistle drank his share. He was an expert plasterer, and she became expertly plastered. People were leaving, bar staff were collecting up glasses, Thistle's head was leaned against George's wife's shoulder. George gently repositioned it against Mick's. "You'll have to get a wheelbarrow for her, mate," said George as he and his wife began their walk home. Mick managed to rouse her and, taking her weight, steered her towards the road. "You had better come back with me – you'll never reach your place and manage two flights." She was still half-asleep. Mick's house was a short distance away. He was glad that he had remained relatively sober otherwise they could have both fallen in the gutter. He managed to herd her up the stairs and shepherd her into a spare bedroom where, with great care, he laid her on the bed. Her arms lay still; she was out for the count. Ice-blonde strands of hair hung across her forehead and her mouth had pulled itself into the rosebud shape of a cupid's bow. He couldn't take his eyes away. Heaven was laid out before him; it was within his power to explore it.

"Goodnight, my angel," whispered Mick as he tenderly covered her with a duvet, turned off the light and left the room, closing the door behind him. As he walked into his bedroom, he knew that he was right to follow his conscience. Work swindles aside, Mick was a man of principles, with a high degree of chivalry.

Morning brought the smell of cigarette smoke, eggs and bacon to Thistle's nostrils. Her eyes, once fully open, looked around a professionally decorated bedroom. *Mick's. I am at Mick's house.* She felt inside her skirt; her knickers were exactly where they should be, undisturbed, in place. Thistle had given the world a chance, but would the world return the compliment? Would she get a 'last chance'?

She found Mick in his kitchen; a cigarette dawdled in an ashtray by an open window. He was bent over a frying pan. He gave her menu choices: "Coffee, tea, eggs – bacon? Hangover pills?"

She squirmed. "Tea please, and yes – hangover pills…"

He threw over a packet of paracetamol.

Thistle noticed the time. "It's gone ten o'clock… oh, Jesus… work – we have to be at work."

"Worry not. I called Don. The whole country has a hangover. He squared it with the homeowner, but it will be a day out of our holiday entitlement. C'mon, girl – get some food in you."

Thereafter the locals from The Wheatsheaf and Don's operatives all presumed that Mick and Thistle were 'in a relationship'. Having seen Thistle from a different perspective, the two young operatives who attended the 'wedding party' and who usually worked together, were callous in their judgement: "What the hell does she see in that old fart?"

"I reckon he's been giving her one all the way along. That's why she's often 'assisting him'." They laughed.

"He needs 'assistance', from what I hear…" Their toilet humour was kept quiet from Don and George. George was wiser than his rough and ready manner would suggest. He said to his wife of thirty-eight years, whom he first met when she was a croupier in a downtown casino, "I hope it works out for young Mickey boy."

"Why do you say that, you old fool?"

"Thistle – she's an odd one."

"Well – odd numbers have an equal probability of turning up in any game of chance."

# 11

# Stardust

MICK AND THISTLE's relationship developed during that August, as she simulated her particular genus of thistle, the Cirsium, which can regenerate from broken pieces and quickly spread in grassland. If Mick was the grass, then his worthiness was a bee seeking nectar from her flower, but not in the way that all around envisaged. In 1980 he had taken a repeat fertility test; sperm count analyses had increased in accuracy since his initial sample was taken in 1975. The result was the same. *I will never be a father.* This rankled, but he kept his disappointment from all who knew him and made the conscious decision never to pursue romance or marriage. 'Women want to be mothers', a belief based on his traditional Greek upbringing, had sealed his fate. On the night of the royal wedding, he quashed once and for all any idea that he could or should harbour even a distant wish for a normal relationship with Thistle. He had fallen in love with her cordial and like an infertile pollinator found himself conditioned to keep hovering; he was destined to elicit and enjoy the part that she secreted even if the extract would remain stagnant. Mick's rationale was based on shielding and nurture. His adaptation was the man he would have been for the child he would never seed, the function of devoted custodian. Life could take 'the man' out of Mick but not Mick out of 'the man'.

Thistle spread her roots and bathed in Mick's dedication. She remembered the feeling of being Venus in Botticelli's painting nine years beforehand. *I was once a Roman goddess and now I am the divine being of a humble Greek, and mortal men are not allowed to touch a goddess.* Adoration was an antiseptic for the abrasions scratched across her self-esteem. During her relationship with Hilary, Thistle had begun to exhume the 'bad' mother of her unconscious, who needed punishing. The mother had to learn what it was like to be crushed into non-existence, to have self-worth ground into powder by pestle and mortar. Yet Thistle had become attached, as a child does to its mother. Attachment isn't always 'attached' to love. She now had a replacement: the once-absent father who Thistle had spent many hours waiting for, yearning to see him walk up the driveway of Chantry House. It was a father's duty to protect his child, to ensure that she survived and thrived. Mick, in loco parentis, facilitated another of Thistle's subliminal fantasies to reach fruition. On Sundays he would drive them to the coast or to the forest for walks, picnics or pub lunches. On Friday evenings he became her escort to the Duke of Wellington; leaning against the bar, he watched male customers with eagle eyes. He did the same at The Wheatsheaf. Thistle no longer needed her own spikes; Mick encased her in barbed wire. None may intrude or come close to the purple petals. He would have accompanied her to the Anchor Inn, but it was her decision that he stay away. Lurking deep inside was still the fraction of hope in reconciliation with Hilary. Mick could not be allowed to jeopardise this. It was highly unlikely that Hilary would frequent the pub, but its locals were her neighbours and gossip travels fast.

Mick continued decorating his house, which Thistle was happy to help with. He had no interest in the postage stamp of paving stones and grass that served as a garden. For her to recreate another floral paradise was a step too far. Memories of past gardens sneaked into her dreams. There was another significant step she was unwilling to take. It was a damp, late August evening which had migrated into autumnal nippiness. They were watching a melodramatic film from the 1950s in Mick's lounge. He said, "The weather's changing already. Winter is not always pleasant for walking or scootering around. Maybe you should move in here – I have two empty bedrooms."

She did not answer. He topped up their whisky glasses. He did not ask again. Her flat was a safe haven from an incomprehensible world, which included Mick. Thistle wanted a father, but on her terms. The original vanished without a word; there was no assurance that the same would not occur. Nevertheless, dependency began to grow on both sides.

For years Mick had been man of few words, but as they walked or drank (a shared hobby) he found himself opening up. He described his family's exodus from Greece, his marriage and divorce. He trusted her with private information, not needing to because she wasn't listening. *I have heard everything about immigrants from Ronnie. I have experienced failed marriage first-hand and nothing he describes is as harrowing as my twenty-four years.* Mick fitted into an equation; it ensured that Thistle's life equalled an aggregate above the lowest common denominator. His own equations failed to produce arithmetical solutions, particularly because as time went by Thistle began to enjoy playing at 'goddess' and sought new acolytes by casting a fishing net, reeling it in and watching her 'catch' wriggle. Adept at when to use eye contact, she aroused the interest of men only to rise above them with wings of derision.

"Why?" Mick asked; he was both jealous and exasperated.

"Why what? What are you talking about?"

"The messages you send out – even to our customers, our householders. Old Mr Collins is falling hard for your enticements; he is a lonely widower... it's cruel. What are you trying to prove? Your irresistibility?"

"You have no right to question what I do. You don't own me, and *you* don't possess *my* charms, more's the pity." Thistle's verbal knife could be pulled from its pouch with no merciful intent.

Mick had become trapped within his own mixed feelings; he had sworn to protect her, but with each of his divulgences he felt that their relationship was shifting towards mutuality. By late September he had lost the impetus to be 'father figure'. It was as if Thistle had sucked all manner of purpose out of him. He was drowning in emotion, and despite her vampirism she was his only buoyancy aid; he had to reach out. It was the third Sunday of the month. They sat beneath one of the forest's ancient oaks with a picnic and two bottles of wine. They could have been any of the couples who were enjoying the forest on that weekend of 'Indian summer'. She was giggling about rationing out the remaining wine. He reached for the bottle and his face came close to her ice-blonde tresses. She felt a slight puff of breath on her neck and then his copper-brown eyes were staring into her sapphire irises. Thistle's giggling stopped, but her mouth remained slightly open. Mick's lips were upon hers, as if suctioned. It was only for a moment. He shrank back.

"I'm s-s-sorry," he stammered. "It must be the wine – it's gone to my head. I don't know what to say."

"Say nothing." Thistle looked into the distance, as if to merge with its greenery, melt away. She waited for the familiar feeling of revulsion to arise from her belly. It didn't. Instead, was the sense of something she was unaccustomed to: humility, affection, truth. Mick's kiss had its origin in love; Thistle felt its honesty.

"Let's forget it, Mick. We are both a bit tipsy."

Neither of them could forget that moment. It was relived in their minds every single day. By Thursday, after four days working together in virtual silence, Mick made the decision to put space between them. He felt it was the gallant thing to do.

On Friday morning George picked her up. "Where's Mick?"

"Had to go somewhere – about his family, I think. Don said Mick would phone you later. By the way, you are working with Vinnie on Monday."

"Why not you?"

"Have to go to wife's aunt's funeral in Scunthorpe or Stockport or somewhere like that. A flipping way to go, so we're staying overnight on Monday to be there for Tuesday morning."

Mick's call came as Thistle returned from work. "I cannot pick you up tonight for the Duke. Sorry it is such short notice, but I have come up to London to see my parents – remember... I told you that they live here with my sister and her family."

Thistle felt her stomach churn. "How long?" She made her enquiry sound casual.

"Not sure. I am owed annual leave so squared it with Don. There's food in the fridge that needs eating if you want to pop in and collect it. Take care, Thistle. Be careful."

She replaced the receiver and reached into her bag for the emotional first-aid kit. The inconceivable had happened: the disciple had walked away from his goddess; the father had left the house. In a wasteland of aloneness both the deity and the child felt their hearts ache. The disciple and the father were more than just mortal men; their love was of the gods. She couldn't face food and was tempted to cancel her session at the Duke, but a need to play the piano overruled her impulse. The moped ride to the city was unsteady, but once sat in front of the piano she felt grounded and stabilised. *Is it too late to drink at the last-chance saloon?* she asked herself as tunes sprung from a wishing-well of throbbing sorrow.

"Play 'For You, Beloved'," yelled out one of the septuagenarian regulars. She did, with a poignancy she had never given it before.

On Saturday evening Mick's sister joined him in the garden as he sank a beer.

"Mommy and Papakis might not notice much, but I do. Come on – what's up?"

"Don't know what you mean. I just thought it was time to pay you all a visit."

"Without saying how long you are staying for? Something is going on; you haven't been like this since *she* left."

"Well – there is no *she* this time. I told you before – I will never have a woman in my life. It isn't fair on them."

"And I have told you – not all women want to be mothers."

"Says she who has had four kiddies."

"Says your big sister who loves you and reads you like a book. We are not in post-war Greece; we are living in the modernist, cutting-edge culture of 1981. Life has moved on. Do you want to end up a sad old soak? Because that's the way you're going. And quit smoking – didn't having pleurisy shake you up?"

"Nagging over?"

His sister kissed him on the cheek. "Unless you wise up, I will nag you to your grave!"

He gave her a hug.

After a weekend of walking, scootering, little sleep and hardly a bite to eat, Thistle was weak and jaded when Vinnie picked her up. This day, like recent days, the sun was lower in the sky. The Indian summer had summoned up autumn and a fresh breeze whipped at leaves that were beginning to turn. The job was to be one of the last exterior maintenance bookings until the spring. It was a sizeable, detached house in its own grounds. Vinnie had put Thistle's ladder in place, she was to start painting fascia boards, but the can of wood stain had little left in it.

"Just use that up and I will get a new pot ready from the van," said Vinnie, being lazy, as he was known to be. He had just begun smoking his fifth fag of the day. It took ten minutes for her to empty the can, then, with can and brush in one hand, she began to descend. Was it her tiredness, the sun belching into her eyes, a sudden gust of wind or that neither she nor Vinnie had checked the ladder? She felt her foot slip and the ladder began to slope to the left. What happened next, she never recalled. Her left hand was still clasping can and brush as the goddess fell from a great height. She felt her body land on something hard but only momentarily – it rolled off. Instinctively she stretched out her right arm, felt contact with the ground and everything went black.

As she came around in an ambulance, her eyes blinked with recognition and closed again. Within this semi-consciousness she believed she had been ambushed by one of her fantasies. Pushed through corridors, inspected, X-rayed and given liquid painkiller, eventually she had the cognisance to put her left hand to her forehead; there was swelling. She was distracted from this by the sensation of soreness all over her body and that someone was encasing her right hand and wrist. Her head lying almost flat, she could not see the application of a plaster cast. Eventually a nurse brought extra pillows and eased Thistle into a sitting position. Her head felt like lead. The nurse gave her a cup of tea and two white tablets.

"I'm in hospital…" Thistle's statement sounded like a question.

"You had a nasty fall, but you will be fine. The doctor will be here to see you soon."

The nurse hurried to a body on the opposite side of the room who was calling out with the tone of someone requesting better table service in a restaurant.

So many questions were running through Thistle's mind. A nursing assistant brought a tray of chopped-up, unappetising food; it reminded her of the meals at Chantry House. A fork was placed into her left hand. Tears began streaming from her eyes. A puffed-up body sitting up on a nearby bed scolded her: "Don't know why you're crying – that woman over there has two broken legs. I heard them say you only got a broken wrist. What do you want… sympathy? Bloody selfish…"

Another nurse appeared and the vixen shut up. Not only had the goddess fallen to earth but now her nose was to be rubbed in its muck. It seemed an eternity until a rotund doctor with the face of a baking potato marched up to Thistle's bed and sat at the bottom.

"You have been in the wars, haven't you?" he said, kindly.

"What happened... am I alright...?" Thistle was blubbering. A nurse gave her a tissue.

The doctor confirmed her trade before explaining assessment, diagnosis and treatment. "I understand that you are a painter and decorator?" He wasn't really asking but his eyes showed puzzlement.

"Yes. I was painting fascia boards – that's the last I remember."

"You fell. The ladder slipped, and you lost your footing. Luckily an apex garage roof broke your fall, but you hit the ground with your right hand taking first impact and your head taking a bounce. Fortunately, it was garden lawn, but you will feel like you have done two rounds with 'Giant Haystacks' for a few days!"

Thistle was annoyed by his jocundity.

He continued, "You have what we call a stable fracture to your right wrist. This makes remedial work easier because if it had been an unstable fracture you would have required surgery. As it is the plaster cast will ensure the bones can reposition. Simple. You have multiple bruising but no other breaks – however you did suffer concussion. Your boss says you live alone?"

"You have spoken with him?"

"He phoned the moment he heard about the accident. Of course I could not tell him anything about your injuries at that point, and without your consent."

"Yes, I do live alone."

"In that case we will definitely keep you in overnight."

Thistle's whimpering had not diminished. "How long do I have to wear the cast? When can I work again? Soon?"

"The cast needs six to eight weeks to do its job, then it will be removed. Afterwards you will need to wear a tubigrip. Realistically you could probably return to work in three months, although it will take a year for appreciable improvement. Physio will be offered, and we will give you a waterproof cast-cover. All being well you will be sent home tomorrow with painkillers, but you will need to obtain more from your GP. It is your right hand, so you will find many tasks extra difficult for a while. I would suggest you ask to stay with a friend or get someone in to help."

"I am left-handed. I was carrying an empty can and a brush in my left hand."

"That's lucky then – and explains why you didn't put your dominant hand out when falling as most people do, and why I assumed your right-handedness. When you do return to work you will find it easier to carry heavy cans in your left hand as the right will be weaker and you won't have as much flexibility."

"I also play the piano… when can I play again?"

The doctor's smile straightened to a flat line. He hesitated. "We would expect that you will be able to play the piano again in the future, but your right hand won't have the manoeuvrability that it had. Your left hand will be okay."

Thistle's woefulness turned to anger. "You don't understand. My left hand is mainly responsible for rhythm – it is my right hand that plays the intricacies."

"I am sorry. I cannot guarantee what level of tractability will return to your right hand. I would hope that eventually you will be able to play, but…" He could not make false promises. "In time suppleness should improve as part of overall healing." He stood up, ready to move on to his next patient, acutely aware that he had just delivered chilling news.

"Please, Doctor… can someone phone my boss and explain about my injury? He will need to reschedule my duties."

Thistle retreated into the shell of her mind's eye. *This is just a dream. I will wake up.*

Don appeared with a bargain box of chocolates at the six o'clock visiting time. He was defensive about how the accident had occurred until Thistle took all responsibility. "The sun was in my eyes, and I slipped, which tipped the ladder a bit."

"Accidents happen in this trade, but by the sounds of it you aren't too injured. Of course, I will keep your job open – I can get a laddie in to assist the guys. You are entitled to two weeks' sick pay – I have insurance to provide this. You will need to apply for government sickness benefit for the rest of the time you can't work. I am sure Mick will help you to do that."

"Mick – does he know?"

"He left me his sister's number in case a major job suddenly came up."

As if on cue Mick rushed into the ward. Don quickly stopped his advance. The two stood in hushed whispers. Don turned towards Thistle and waved goodbye. Mick ignored an uncomfortable visitor's chair and sat himself on the side of the bed. His breathing was irregular and his face distraught.

"I thought I told you to be careful…?" Tears glistened from what were now the eyes of a disconsolate spaniel.

"I'm sorry... I..." Thistle could neither unearth nor verbalise words which lay beneath layers of past pretence, theatricals and compulsive contrivance. *This wasn't a plot to get you back.* He read her remorse.

"It's my fault. I shouldn't have gone away. If George or I were with you it wouldn't have happened. We always check ladders, positioning... what time of day is best for an angle which avoids looking into the sun. If you had started on the other side of the house... or at least worn a cap."

"I knew that. I have worked with you and George long enough. I forgot my cap and I couldn't face confronting Vinnie – he told me where to start and I didn't want an argument which would end with the mockery of: 'You're just an assistant.'"

"Trouble is, he fancies you and wants to prove his manhood by exerting authority – that's how some men are. Let's be thankful you weren't more badly hurt."

"Mick – I might not ever be able to play the piano properly again." Her eyes welled up.

He dabbed her cheeks. "You will, you are a very single-minded lady – think positive. In the meantime, you aren't going to be able to work."

"I know. Don explained about sickness benefit. He said you would help me with the forms."

"Thistle... the amount of sickness benefit you will get won't cover the rent on your flat and living expenses. You may be eligible for another benefit, but it still won't be enough to live on for three months; Don has just filled me in."

The goddess's world was slipping through her fingers. The land on which she lay became quicksand; she clung to its crumbling edge while sinking further into a mire.

"What am I going to do?" After all the years of grit and determination Thistle was once again a piteous eight-year-old child.

"Move in with me." Mick's words were as plain as the man who spoke them. In guessing her thoughts, he added, "I won't touch you."

She extended her left arm across her body to make contact between her left hand and his right hand, which was resting on the bed. Only the previous day she had asked the universe, *Is Mick the man I could fall in love with?* Then she had murmured the final words of 'For You, Beloved': "And there's a chance of love staying – love staying... forever."

How long is 'forever'? It is infinity for a body in recovery. Infinity is an impossible concept; therefore the only way to deal with it is by denial: *The injury cannot last for that long; the medical profession always give the worst-case scenario; I will be back to normal in no time.*

Whilst Mick tied on the pinafore of 'mother hen', arranging the largest spare bedroom to create a Thistle-friendly space, moving her belongings out of the flat, even scootering her moped over and installing it in his garage, she pumped herself full of prescription drugs in anticipation of that day, which would soon arrive, when life would return to normality. She wasn't the only one in denial. When Mick went to the pharmacy for painkillers, Thistle asked him to take her next prescription for tranquilisers. He did not know she had been popping those for months. "Painkillers and tranquilisers? Is that wise?"

"I need them, Mick – I have anxiety, which is even worse now."

He did not argue. He could not refuse her anything, which included alcohol, strictly forbidden whilst on the painkillers.

"Maybe you shouldn't drink with all these tablets?"

"I need to, Mick – I have to feel 'up', sometimes."

The alcohol did not act as an 'upper'; it merely increased the subterranean level of despondency into which she was plummeting. Mick began to feel inadequate; no matter what he suggested Thistle wore a cloak of misery.

"I will drive you out to the forest for a walk – that will lift your spirits."

"It's too cold and wet."

"How about we go to Calford-on-Sea… have chips overlooking the—"

She quickly interrupted, "No point. Sea mist – we won't see a thing, and chips are just fatty fingers of stodge."

"Nearer the time when you can start to play piano, I will buy one for you."

"Your house is too small."

"I can fit one in. I will move the sideboard upstairs."

"Jesus, Mick, don't you realise – I will *never* be able to play, so *don't* waste your money."

She ran upstairs, slammed the bedroom door and threw a biography of Vivien Leigh onto the floor. Thistle remembered herself as a young child, when she would spend hours working out nursery rhymes of guileless gaiety. Tunefulness became solace. As the years went by, musical invention unleashed her pent-up creativity, generated from the blanket of agony that life had swaddled her in. Thistle pounded the fingers of her left hand against an unresponsive door and recalled the satisfaction of pressing a piano key and hearing the note she wanted to produce singing back to her. That was power. It was creating a melody for all to enjoy, especially herself. She looked at her partially hidden right hand. A segment of her that she no longer owned or controlled. For most of her life, by hook or by crook, she had managed to access a piano through different homes, schools, or pubs. *The mountain came to Mohammed*, she said to herself. *But now Mohammed cannot get to the mountain. Jesus Christ – is this how God shows his love?* The paradox of religion ignited a fuse. Inwardly she shouted, *And this is not karma, Ronnie's mother – you stupid woman. I don't deserve to be punished this way. Your spoiled son grew up with expectations beyond his class or know-how; his karma is – not to fulfil yours! Even Hilary admitted that it wasn't my fault to have been abused and abandoned... Hilary...* Thistle imagined Hilary's less-than-talented hands wafting over piano keys, producing the wooden recital of a composer's ingenuity. *Stuffy, staid Hilary. She'll have her comeuppance when the boyfriend vanishes, leaving her heart sagging from its frayed washing line.* The thought of Hilary reminded Thistle of Fliss. *What a waste of breath she is... always talking, constantly chipper, thinking she is queen of the kitchen. I bet she's lying under a table conjoined with a*

*bottle of brandy, whilst some chevalier has his wicked way.*
*She'll get what she deserves – with luck, syphilis.*

Internalised anger can result in depression. Thistle
was launching rockets of rage towards the world as she
knew it, but they bounded back from deaf walls, to
impale themselves on the monstrosity of her perceptions.
Figurative imprisonment. Later she appeared downstairs as
Mick was preparing dinner.

"Mick – I am sorry. It isn't your fault. You are doing
so much to try to make me happy, but right now I am in a
dungeon."

"I know you are. Hold on. We will get there. *You* will
get there. This time will pass, but while it is going by, please
eat more."

Food had become another issue. Having lived alone for
a few years Mick was a reasonable cook. Thistle's appetite
had never been large but now food spent more time being
pushed around her plate than finding its way into her
mouth.

After fourteen days Mick had to return to work.
He would have taken unpaid holiday, but an insurance
company had given the go-ahead for a job which required
much re-plastering. He was concerned about leaving Thistle
alone. Out of her hearing he phoned George and asked if
his wife could pop in occasionally. Then he called Ruth.
Thistle had not wanted Ruth to know about the accident; he
could not understand why. Ruth was upset to hear the news
and promised to visit. Thistle realised that George's wife
was checking up on her. The only saving grace was George's
wife telling stories of her time as a croupier. Decades later,

shaped similarly to George's rugby-ball figure, with permed white hair and pink jowls, Thistle found it darkly comical to imagine her as svelte, bejewelled and glamourous. Her other use was in changing Thistle's library books. Mick pre-warned Thistle of when Ruth would arrive. She thought of leaving the house, but it started raining. Ruth had left the baby with her mother so that she could devote her attention to Thistle. There was no pre-warning to Ruth about the woman she found languishing on a sofa. She had not seen Thistle for at least two months. The weight loss was concerning, as were rings under her eyes and the pallor of her skin.

"Oh, Thistle. What is happening to you? You have always been skinny, but now you are gaunt. Should you be living here? Who is this man? Is he feeding you? Are you safe here?"

"Stop, Ruth… please. It isn't Mick's fault. He is good, kind and loves me. I just need to build my strength up. I will be fighting fit again soon – just wait and see." Thistle's attempts at cheerfulness did not convince Ruth.

"He loves you? You are in a relationship? You said you were seeing someone ages ago. I assumed it was a…"

"A woman?"

"Yes. So, do you actually love this man or is he a means to an end?"

"Ouch, Ruth – that hurt."

"Sorry, but you forget how long I have known you."

"I am not absolutely sure how I feel. That is the truth, but no, he isn't a pawn on my chessboard. Once I feel better then maybe I will be ready to pursue a proper relationship."

"You aren't sleeping with him then?"

"No."

Ruth sensed a no-go area. Changing the subject, she unwittingly stepped into another. "Have you let Hilary know about your accident?"

"Definitely not."

"Why? I don't know what you two argued about, but I am sure she would still want to be your friend."

"No – she would not. She's tangled up with a married man. All I did was point out that she would end up hurt, and she flew off the handle. She's become quite irrational."

Thistle's interpretation of past events had always been spurious, re-framed to minimise any fault on her part but in turn maximise the imperfection in others.

Ruth promised to visit again. Conversation had tired Thistle; she climbed the stairs and lay on her bed. Their dialogue repeated itself over and over again. *A proper relationship – that meant a sexual relationship.* Recently this subject had begun to annexe Thistle's pre-sleep thoughts. Every night while lying awake in the dial light of an alarm clock, she would play it out in her head: how it would be to share Mick's bed. *When I am better,* she told herself, *he will be gentle. I will feel cherished. It will be a natural outpouring of our love. Heaven will smile and all the devils will be shooed away. We will find contentment, and a flurry of confetti will fall from the ether. I will be the most adoring wife and live happily ever after.*

Losing oneself in romantic Hollywood films and the glossed-over biographies of their frequently conflicted heroines, is the perfect way to avoid confronting reality.

For Hilary to have become irrational would be for Thatcher's government to have declared trade unions victorious in the political amphitheatre of employment rights. Ruth thought about ringing her, but Jed advised against it: "Don't jump in that dinghy, love – it's likely to capsize."

As it was, Hilary already knew. A neighbour who was an Anchor Inn regular told Hilary how her ex-lodger had fallen and broken her wrist. "Can't play for months, so I heard. Mind you, I knew a bloke who never played again after breaking his. Shame, eh?"

Hilary knew the severity of emotional reaction that being unable to play the piano would invoke. She phoned the number she had for the flat, but of course there was no reply. She tried again: no answer. She spoke to Charles; he said, "She has your number, I am sure she would phone if she needed anything. I feel sorry for her, especially about the piano, but since she has gone you are a different person. Had you realised that? You are confident and decisive. You are eating up the training and other opportunities that the library service keep throwing at you. Hilary – you are going for life and making a success of it. I wouldn't want anyone, including me, to hold you back."

✿

Mick persevered with encouraging Thistle to eat and in doing so he achieved stabilisation. She remained underweight. He would also not give up on bringing the world to her as she increasingly attempted to withdraw. On

Thursday November 5th he wrapped her in a bedspread and drove them to a hill above the eastern side of Bistead, from where they could watch innumerable firework displays rising from gardens and local parks: a host of missiles hell-bent on winning a race to reach the moon. He held her left hand; the once-stumpy fingers now felt like tentacles.

"I will get better," she said. He was deeply worried. The following Monday he tried to speak with her doctor but was told that as he was not next of kin, Thistle's right to confidentiality could not be breached. On the same day her decree nisi arrived in the post. After work he found it screwed up into a ball on the kitchen table. He spread it out and added it to a folder he was creating of her personal documents, which he had found randomly stuffed into a Sainsbury's carrier bag. Some items he clipped together in chronological order. Bank statements were separated out into a different file. In doing this he came across her birth certificate: 'Karen Agnetha Kristensen, born Fifteenth of March, Nineteen Fifty-Seven'.

*Who could give this child away?* For a moment sadness turned to fury in the man who would never be a biological father. *Adopt*, he thought, *we could adopt if we were married.* Immediately he took these ideas to Thistle.

"I have been thinking – I would never want you to be in the position of having no home again, plus if you had another accident or illness, you need a person who can speak with the medical profession."

She looked up from a biography of Marilyn Monroe.

He continued, "It won't be long before your decree absolute comes through." Then he stumbled over his words:

"It's just… well, the answer to ensuring that you are always safe and secure is for you to… to… I am making a hash of this. Thistle – I cannot give you children, not of our own, but we could adopt, if we were…"

"Married?" She saved him from his uneasiness.

He dropped to one knee in a gentlemanly pose. "Will you please become my wife?"

"And will we live happily ever after?"

"I think so. I hope so. I love you so much, you must know that by now."

She knew. She had embraced the same idea in her fairy tales, but it was an honest Thistle who replied, "I am honoured that you want to marry me – I could not ask for more – but until I feel well, I cannot contemplate what the future might look like. Please wait for me, Mick, I cannot give you an answer right now."

He really wasn't her pawn, and she was not about to take advantage of him in any way. Proof indeed of her capability to 'love'.

There are days and dates which are forever imprinted on our memories. Friday November 20th 1981 was never erased from Mick's. Only the day before Thistle seemed happier; the appointment for her cast to be removed had come through the post. It was for the following Tuesday and signified the first major step towards normality. Underneath her flaky joy lie a tightly strapped agitation; it was also a way-marker on the road to determining how much elasticity her wrist would be left with. Would she ever again be master of the ivories, or would they outwit, outsmart and demolish her? This dire deliberation sparked fear. The future was unknown, but it contained that all-consuming dread: there would never again be catharsis at the keys.

On Friday 20th there was a major accident on the city-centre ring-road. Mick and the lad Don had hired to replace Thistle had been working west of the city. They sat for nearly two hours in bumper-to-bumper traffic whilst flashing lights and sirens brought chaos to both highway and night sky. Eventually Mick dropped the lad off and sped home. Thistle was asleep on the sofa. He touched her arm. "Wakey, wakey. Sorry I am late – dreadful accident on the inner ring-road but better to be stuck in a traffic jam than be part of the crash."

Her arm fell limp at the side of the sofa. On a nearby coffee table lay empty tablet packets, the biography of Marilyn Monroe and remains of a bottle of wine. "Thistle..." He lifted her shoulder – it fell back. The one fact he never remembered was how long he stood there, looking, waiting for her eyes to open, but at some point he noticed a piece of paper which had fallen to the floor in between the sofa and the coffee table. In Thistle's handwriting, it read:

*Mick – I decided to write my own song. I have a tune in my head, so if I am able to play the piano again, I can play it to you:*

*"At the end of the day, I look in the mirror and see myself*
*At the end of the day, the only one I must face is myself*
*The decisions I've made, right or wrong, those decisions were mine*
*The decisions I tried, failed or succeeded; they also were mine.*

"And the hurt that I feel was probably never intended to be
This hurt that I feel is something of value, a large part of
    me.

"At the end of the day, while closing my eyes, I shut out
    my life
At the end of the day, like stardust I fall from dark starry
    skies
The person I am, switched off with the light, closed out by
    the door
 At the end of the day, there is only me, nothing less,
    nothing more."

Mick, it feels like I am floating on stardust, surrounded by
    moonbeams,
and I love you.

# 12

# From a Distance

A POST-MORTEM AND inquest were carried out. The medical findings were clinical and convoluted. Her body weight was a significant factor. The testimony of character witnesses, who stated that Thistle had been in a good state of mind and positive about the future, were entered into the record. In short, the conclusion was: "Heart failure brought about by an accidental overdose of prescription drugs." Whether it was accidental or deliberate only one person knew and she was no longer on earth to tell anyone. If it was suicide, then was it an act of mercy? To save Mick from the toxicity that, although recently negligible, could have seeped out of Thistle if the circumstances warranted it. Or was Mick to pay the ultimate price in penance for the father who had disappeared? His unconditional love had been trawling through previously unexplored terrain – her capacity to return it. Had he invaded the long grass of her psyche only to prick his finger on the barbs of a wounded heart? Did she know that the only way to successfully exterminate a thistle is with chemicals? If so, she applied her own weedkiller. Mick would spend the rest of his life regretting that he did not put lethal compounds out of reach. The boy had been taken away from Greece, but archetypal tragedy had followed, to become his life's script.

In the days immediately following her death Mick was in the first stage of grief: shock with disbelief. This carried him until Tuesday when, having dealt with formalities, he began to shake with uncontrollable morbidity. He phoned Ruth to tell her of Thistle's death. She, like everyone else on hearing the news, had to confront her own giant of guilt. Each person felt that they could have done more. Ruth reproached herself for having not visited more often – perhaps Thistle wouldn't have become so dependent on substances had her friends been more 'dependable'. Ruth suggested he call Hilary. That evening Mick plucked up the courage to phone 'the mad woman'. After two minutes of speaking with her he knew that Hilary was definitely not loony, potty or unstable. After introducing himself and relating the devastating news, she had to balance herself by holding on to a door handle. Then Hilary could hear that he was beyond being an understandably broken man – he was shattered glass, splintered into one thousand fragments. "I don't know what to do… what to do… her things, her clothes… inquest… funeral." His voice was that of a newly born lamb bleating for its mother. Despite shockwaves running through her body, Hilary knew she had to take charge and asked for Ruth's number; Hilary could carry the responsibility, but not on her own. Mick was clutching crumbs of equilibrium.

"I'm going up to London... my family. I will leave a key under the back-door mat. Do you mind... you don't even know me?"

"It's alright. I understand. You need to be with those who love you... please leave me your number up there and... I am so sorry."

Next it was Hilary's turn to mentally collapse on someone; she looked at the clock, registering that it would be a suitable time to phone Fliss.

"I have killed Thistle."

"Good God – what are you talking about?"

"She fell off a ladder—"

"Did you push her?"

"No. It was an accident at work – at the beginning of October. She fell off a ladder and broke her wrist."

"Then how on earth have you killed her?"

"I was told about it, and I phoned her flat; there was no reply. I phoned again, and then I left it. I made no more effort. Don't you see – I was the only person to understand what being unable to play the piano, plus the prospect of never again playing properly, would be doing to her. I even did some research into pianists with hand injuries; they often become depressed. Playing the piano is their emotional outlet – they cannot survive without it. Thistle overdosed last Friday. It isn't yet clear whether it was accidental. I could have done more to contact her. I knew where she worked. I didn't try. It is my fault she is dead, because I knew how bizarre her behaviour could become when she felt angst-ridden – towards others but also towards herself."

"I don't understand. What do you mean?"

Hilary had to explain about the Panda incident. Fliss's French blood began to boil.

"Now listen to me, Hilary – it is not your fault. She was obviously not in control of herself. Let me know when the funeral is – I will come over."

"You want to come to her funeral?"

"Yes. Partly for her, but mostly for you."

As Fliss put the phone down Mat was at her side.

"Mat, I will have to go to England."

"What's happened? Your face is as white as a sheet."

"Someone I knew has died." Fliss was staring up at the ceiling. "I wasn't always kind to her in life, but it is more than that – I want to support Hilary."

"Yes, of course. I'll help Francine with Le Pommier. What are you looking up at?"

"Angels – I hope. Mat, can you come to the church with me? I want to light a candle."

As they drove in darkness to Pont l'Eveque an owl flew right in front of the windscreen. Fliss watched it wing away into trees which were now naked of foliage.

❧

On Saturday morning Hilary met Ruth outside Mick's house. Both felt uncomfortable to enter his home and neither were equipped to manage their emotions when they began to sort through Thistle's few possessions. Like Mick, they both had a barricade of disbelief separating themselves from reality. Before long they were both crying. Hilary found the matching hat, gloves and scarf set she had given Thistle the previous Christmas. She remembered their walk and sitting by the harbour.

"Ruth, did you know that Thistle was sexually assaulted when she was only eight years old?"

"Oh, my word – no. I didn't. How can anyone do that… to a child?" Ruth's voice was muffled by sniffles. She came across an illustrated bible, designed for children. Inside was the inscription: "To our dearest, darling Karen. Love from Mummy and Daddy." The sobbing continued. Out of the bible fell three photographs. Two were in black and white: Thistle – one when she was aged eighteen months, the other at seven years. In both were tumbles of corkscrew curls framing the face of a cherub. The third was a photo of a scrawny, grey-haired couple in their sixties, standing in front of a vibrant, multi-coloured herbaceous border. On the back Thistle had written: "Eric and Vida – August 1972."

"I cannot bear this," said Hilary as she collected up Thistle's library books. "I'll return these. If it is okay with you, we could share out the bags of clothing and take them to charity and second-hand shops. There's not much…"

Ruth was still grizzling. Hilary picked up a marbled box out of the top drawer of a bedside table. Inside, on a nest of cottonwool sat two rings; both were white gold, but one was studded with a sapphire. "Marriage – another toll of the bell."

Hilary had now moved into abject melancholy. Through her tears she spluttered, "I will ask Mick if he wants the bible and photos – almost all that remains of twenty-four years of life. But I don't think he will want these rings."

"They should be buried with her." From under the bed Ruth pulled out a portable radio-cassette player and a shoe box full of music tapes, some classical, others spanning decades of popular songs.

"Do you think Mick will want these? He has a hi-fi system downstairs."

"We will ask him. We will also have to talk to him about the funeral – where he wants her buried."

Ruth blew her nose. "I can organise that. My dad is vicar of St Mark's in the city centre, and my brother is curate of Bistead parish church; he joined 'the family business'. Thistle lived this side of the city since she left the house that we both had bed-sits in. I will ask my brother to conduct the service in the parish church – if Mick agrees."

*A vicar's daughter*, acknowledged Hilary. *That explains her coupling of rebelliousness and altruism.*

Shared grief can act as a hinge of connectivity between people. That hinge was well lubricated on Saturday morning as Hilary and Ruth organised, bagged up and cried over relics of Thistle: verification that she had once lived. A bond was formed between two women from religious backgrounds. It grew into a lasting friendship.

Hilary bundled books and bags into her 1978 ochre-coloured Mini. She had passed her test in September and found the ideal vehicle at a used car sales business in Ashbrook. Her parents gave her some money towards it; there was, as always, 'a catch'.

"We are getting on," began her mother. "There will come a time when perhaps neither I nor your dad will be able to drive, then we will need you to take us shopping, for days out and hospital appointments, so it's best you become an experienced driver before we have to be your passengers."

Hilary had eyed her mother with suspicion; was it their plan to have had a third child in their later years in order to be sure of continued service and care? Nevertheless, the money helped her to buy a car which was only three years old and ran like a dream. She did not attend the inquest as she had not seen Thistle for five months and could not comment on her mental health. Ruth, George, his wife and Don attended. Don read out Mick's written statement. It said that Mick had asked her to marry him, and that Thistle had more or less agreed to do so once she was better. Everyone assumed this referred to her wrist 'getting better'. Hence the coroner's verdict of accidental death. She had been looking to the future with a sound mind.

Winter is not such a bad time to die. In England so much around us is already deceased: deciduous leaves, bedding plants and flowering heads. Perennials have often disappeared into the soil, hibernating until the spring. Even the sun spends more of its life dead in the sky. Thistle had been a spring baby and was now a winter's cadaver, not so different from living human beings who scuttle indoors on winter days, like corpses falling into coffins. Her coffin sat at the front of the church, its rigidity softened by wreaths. The mortal remains contained within were as invisible to the eye as the body's soul. Where had Thistle's soul gone? Was it still a young, white, female spirit? Does a soul change its age, shape, gender and colour? Is it judged? Does it find a kindred spirit? Is the soul a definitive shape, gender or colour whilst it still inhabits the body? Most people would answer, "Of course not." Funeral services celebrate the life of the soul, its time on earth, then according to which religion one follows its post-death destination is concluded as a matter of covenant. Ask no questions. If Thistle's soul were watching her funeral from a distance, what would she have noticed? That people were there for her in death yet not in life? That there were mourners present who had tried to love her, even if only one had succeeded?

Her savings would not have covered the funeral costs and coffin; Don coughed up the rest. He felt it was the least he could do. Don was currently facing a dilemma. Vinnie had left his employ under a cloud. Mick had told Don of his intention to sell up and move to London, and 'old' George was due to retire in a few months. It was imperative that these latter two, highly skilled operatives, train up new staff. So, the previous day Don had placed an advertisement in the local paper: "Trainee Painter/ Decorator Operatives Required. Applications welcome from Men *and* Women."

"It would be fitting to encourage more girls into the trade," he told his wife. "And I will ensure that no-one will be ranked as just an assistant, so that all operatives of either sex start on the same wages."

Sat together were what appeared to be identical twins. They were in fact the publican cousins of the Duke of Wellington and the Anchor Inn.

"I never increased her fee, even when her beret didn't pull in the coins. Did you?"

"No – I figured she enjoyed playing for the sake of it."

"Did you send her flowers when she broke her wrist?"

"No – did you?"

"No. Pubs are busy places. I meant to visit her, but… you know how it is."

Someone Thistle might have expected to be paying their respects was Ronnie. Their decree absolute had recently and legally ended the marriage after her death had achieved the same. On this spartan December day Ronnie was stood side by side with a woman who was pregnant with their child. They were attending the city's registry office. He had a buttonhole. She had a spray of winter-flowering camellia entwined with nerines and viburnum tinus. Ronnie's mother had been florist.

Ruth read the eulogy. It took her a long time to write because she did not know what to say. It was not a protracted tribute. She had made efforts to 'love' Thistle as a friend on numerous occasions, but Thistle rarely reciprocated the same level of fondness. In May Ruth's baby had taken precedence, which is the way of the world. Thistle's 'inner baby' could not compete. This fanned the flame of acrimony which raised Thistle's temperature to levels of nastiness which Ruth found hard to ignore. There was also the Jed effect. He tolerated Thistle for Ruth's sake, but Jed knew what Ruth did not want to admit – that Thistle turned up when she wanted something or had nothing else better to do. Thistle had not seen Jed for some time. She would have been tickled to see him with a 'short back and sides' haircut and wearing a conventional suit. Crafting rugs and mosaics wasn't bringing in enough for a family of three; Jed got a job in insurance. The funeral service was conducted with Ruth's minimalist style. She had instructed her brother in this. "There will be a great deal of raw emotion – keep it low-key." She knew her brother; his natural stoicism would read from the book of God with ceremonial impassiveness. Hilary read out a Buddhist poem about a butterfly. She had never had any indication that Thistle was Christian, and Christianity was a controversial subject for Hilary.

"A butterfly – my butterfly, for a while."

Thistle may have been surprised to see Fliss present, but she would have correctly guessed that Fliss's main object was to support Hilary. Thistle's jealousy had prevented her making the same level of friendship with Fliss as Hilary enjoyed. Are souls still jealous as they sweep their eyes over the congregation? Whom in this case were now singing a hymn: 'Abide with Me'. Mick's choice. Within a continued state of anguish his prayer was that God would abide by Thistle in death, as he had ostensibly not bothered to in life. Mick hung on to the belief that Thistle's overdose was accidental. The alternative was refused entry into his mind. Next to Mick sat a black-haired woman in her forties. She was gripping his hand like a mother in fear that her child will run out under a car. Would Thistle have realised she was Mick's sister? If Thistle had listened to his history, then she might have.

George and his missus sat near the back of the church, their tubby forms filling a three-person pew. While they were waiting for the service to begin 'Missus' whispered in George's ear, "If you are ever in the bookies with Mick – *don't* back the same horse that he does. And please advise him never to play Russian roulette." To a croupier an understanding of 'chance' becomes second nature. Behind the two rugby balls, masked by shadows, stood someone else. This person did not sit down; a pillar obscured them from view. Thistle would not have noticed who it was from the heights her soul had now reached, a platform from which she could never fall again.

The moment the coffin was lowered into its consecrated plot the audience quickly dispersed. Mick nodded towards Hilary as he and his sister traversed gravestones, finding the quickest route back to the church carpark. Ruth had a few words with him, then she and Jed did the same. Ruth urgently needed to hold their baby daughter in her arms and feel the optimism that neoteric life brings. Hilary thanked Ruth's brother and he made his escape; he had a phobia of graveyards. Hilary and Fliss were still stood near the grave when the 'shadow figure' arrived and looked into the depths, oblivious to their presence. He had been dawdling amongst taciturn tombs, keen to avoid anyone recognising who he could be. A man in his mid-forties, with receding ice-blond hair flecked with grey. From a sinewy, chiselled face shone arresting blue eyes, now jugs pouring tears.

"He looks like Richard Widmark," said Fliss to Hilary. They looked at each other.

"But it isn't, is it?" replied Hilary. "There's only one person he can be."

They walked towards him but respected his moment of mourning, as did the grave-fillers.

"My darling Karen. My innocent baby girl. I can't believe you are gone… I am so…" His words were throttling him. "If I had known… I loved you, sweetheart. Daddy always loved you." He became aware of their presence.

Hilary held out her hand. "Mr Kristensen, we are so sorry for your loss."

He took her hand in both of his. "I lost my little girl over sixteen years ago, but thank you. And thank you for the poem you read. I am glad she had some friends."

Hilary's guilt complex prodded her sharply in the gut. She made no reply.

"And thanks also to whoever put the death notice in the paper; without that I may never have found her, even though I am too late…" His face creased into ruts of sheer torment.

"There's a bench just here," said Fliss. "Would you like to tell us about it – about Karen? You had been looking for her?"

They all sat down, and the man told his story. Some parts were a little incoherent, but Fliss and Hilary listened patiently.

"I suppose it starts with the situation at the time – 1956, when I met Karen's mother. She was just sixteen; I was twenty-two. I took advantage of her on a 'one-night stand'. I am guessing you two are both in your mid-twenties. Your memories will be of the 'swinging sixties' – well, that era white-washed the wilderness that was the 1950s. Post-war regeneration wasn't achieved overnight. There were many struggles, especially of the emotional kind. In a frenzied act of lust Karen was conceived. The baby would be born before her mother's seventeenth birthday and both our sets of parents were furious. Having completed my National Service I had begun training as an aircraft engineer but was told in no uncertain terms that I must marry the girl and find well-paid work. I gave up my training and ended up in the docks. That would have been alright except the baby's mother did not want to be with me. Her parents had told her that they wouldn't look after her if she chose not to marry me; the baby would therefore have to be put up for adoption. So we married, rented a house and she never spoke to her parents again. Ours was an unhappy relationship from day one. I do not excuse my behaviour – we had violent rows that no child should have witnessed. The relationship with my parents deteriorated – I blamed them, and we began having stand-up verbal fisticuffs. When Karen was two years old they let me have what was 'my' piano and told me to stay out of their lives. As it turned out the piano was the only good thing to have come out of my warring family; Karen showed talent from the moment she could sit on my lap and tap the keys. Before long she would climb onto the piano stool and play for ages. By 1965 I knew I had to leave – for Karen and her mother's sake. After one wretched fight I packed my bags and left. I could not face continuing to work in the docks; I found employment with a shipping line as pianist and singer on their cruise liners which operate from this port."

Both Fliss and Hilary gasped. Hilary voiced their thoughts. "You have been on the cruise liners... all this time… using the estuary. Thistle – sorry, I mean Karen, loved watching the cruise ships. For years she walked the estuary and never knew that you were so close by…"

"You must be able to play the piano well," said Fliss, keen to move conversation on from Hilary's memory of Thistle pacing the estuary path, the warped knot of coincidence that this image evoked.

"I used to play pubs and clubs over the forest way – where my family lived. I continued after marrying Karen's mother, it supplemented our income. Karen inherited her musicality from me."

Hilary began to probe. "She also inherited your looks. I realise you were away at sea a lot of the time, but, and I am sorry to ask this, why did you never visit Karen in the children's home?"

"Because I did not know that she was in one, and I would never have known until eighteen months ago, when I bumped into her mother in a docklands pub. I asked how Karen was getting on to be informed that she had put her into care straight after I had gone. She said she saw Karen briefly the following Christmas, after which the girl refused to see her. My ex-wife's excuse was that she couldn't cope, and that Karen reminded her of me. Karen's mother was only twenty-four years old when I left – I guess she wanted to start a new life, but I had to restrain myself from thumping her when I learned of what she had done."

"The same age as Karen is… I mean, was," observed Fliss.

"I know you must think it uncaring – that I had not tried to contact Karen before – but when I left in 1965, I was a man cultivated by outmoded, obsolete male conventions. I thought that Karen and her mother would be better off without me. I assumed that a decent chap would come along and if I turned up it would cause trouble. I was horror-struck to discover that Karen had been put in a children's home. Even when I received divorce papers no-one mentioned Karen – or where she was. No wonder I wasn't asked for financial contributions. For the past year and a half every time I have been on shore, I have tried to track Karen down. Social services were no help at all. They have taken over the management of Chantry House, but no staff remain from when Karen was there. The foster parent still living has dementia. The last record social services could offer was when they put Karen in a grotty bed-sit when she was sixteen. I know it was grotty because I went to see it. Karen left it years ago – no-one in social services knew where she went, and no-one told me that Karen was known as Thistle. I put an advert in 'missing persons' but nobody came forward."

Hilary spoke. "People tend not to look at those very closely and only Ronnie would have known her maiden name. I know Ruth never knew it, or that her real Christian name was Karen."

"I didn't know she had married. If I had not seen the funeral notice, which cited both birth names, I may never have found her. But I am too late. Too late to say I am sorry. Too late to keep her alive." He wiped his nose on an over-sized handkerchief.

"I put her birth names in the death notice," admitted Hilary, "in hope that a family member may come forward from somewhere. Perhaps it would have been better for you never to have found her; you could have imagined the life she may have been leading."

"No – I deserve the pain I am feeling."

"Her mother deserves to be feeling the same way. She hasn't even attended her funeral."

"I doubt she knows. She wasn't good at reading and hardly looked in a newspaper. The last I heard she was with a sailor. I think they moved to Plymouth. I cannot blame her, not really. She did not ask to get pregnant; she did not want to be with me and, if I am honest, a part of me knew that she was not enjoying motherhood."

"What was Karen like as a little girl?"

His voice mellowed. "She was the dearest child, so sweet and caring. A 'Friday's child' – loving and giving. She looked upon the world as if it were a land of enthralling mystery, which should be safely delighted in. But the world of our family home fell noticeably short of that… the rows, the tension. It affected her, I am sure." His tone dropped. "Now she is an empty husk, and it is all my fault. I was responsible for her birth and now I feel accountable for her death."

"Please, Mr Kristensen, do not take it all on your shoulders. There are things you need to know about Karen's life. Specifically one event which occurred before you left."

He looked perplexed by Hilary's words. She took his hand. "Shall we all go and have a cuppa? There's a tea shop down the road." Fliss nodded in agreement.

As they walked away Fliss felt that they were being watched. She wheeled around to be confronted by a throng of faces. They peeped out from billowing cloud formations, from the gnarled bark of tree trunks and from silhouettes created by their bare branches. "Are you looking down on us, Thistle? Or communing with the other souls? Let your soul rest in peace. At long last allow yourself harmony and union." Turning back to join the others, Fliss was halted by a thought: *Good God, I am becoming Great-Aunt Amelie – conversing with spirits.*

# Epilogue

# August Bank Holiday 1982

HILARY RAN UP the driveway to greet her special friend. Together they entered the maisonette and Fliss poked her nose around. "You have been decorating."

"I never did like the peach paint. Light moss green is so much more soothing. I am not going to strip the wallpaper off the bedroom walls, though – it does look quite nice. How is your new nephew?"

The reason for Fliss's visit to England was to see Philip's son, born two weeks beforehand. The two discussed babies.

"And I see your bump is beginning to show." Hilary studied Fliss's stomach.

Fliss laughed. "Is it? I thought I still had my hour-glass figure!"

"Pregnant but not married – what do your parents say?"

"Oh, you know them – they gave up on me years ago!

No – they are the best parents ever. I am only sorry I did not realise it for my first quarter of a century. They know that Mat and I will tie the knot at some point when we are not so busy. They love him, especially his sense of humour – which is always tempered with kindness."

"When you brought him over, I thought, *What a little treasure* – he will need that sense of humour to cope with you!" Hilary made the sound of a strangled parrot. "But the most important thing is that *you* love him."

"No doubt of that. You were so right, Hilary. I stopped looking and nine months later the last type of person on earth I thought I would ever fall for meanders into my life."

"Will you marry before giving birth? I would like some notice before I actually travel abroad for the first time."

"It depends on how our new ventures pan out."

"Tell me properly – your last letter was a jumble of nonsense, probably due to the morning sickness."

"Ha, that's true! Poor old Didier couldn't cope with even thinking about all my plans for expansion, and he did not really need Mat's help anymore. So, Mat and I began looking around at run-down, failing campsites. We found the perfect one, near Concarneau on the Breton coast. Oh, Hilary, the position is stunning. It has a dilapidated restaurant area with views to the horizon, and the currently slimy swimming pool also overlooks the sea. The whole site and amenities need a lot of loving care and repair but also quite a bit of money to provide that. Mat got us a business loan and from October 1st it is all ours. We are so excited! We can get it up to scratch during the winter ready for next year's holiday season. The elderly proprietors also rented a boutique unit within the medieval walled town, so we have taken that on too. It also needs an overhaul, but I can sort it out – with Francine's help. That will provide us with interim income and a 'fall back'. Didier's eldest daughter is going to manage Le Pommier and Francine is moving into the wonderfully spacious campsite owner's gite with us."

"She has become like a kid sister to you."

"Very much, and do you know, Hilary, I always envied you having a sister. I know my mother has been loving and attentive all my life in contrast to your own, but I hated only having brothers. I would love to have had a sister like your Monica."

"Instead, you are the '*big* sister'?"

"Err – yes and I must soon push Francine down the Hilary road of 'straight and narrow', except that you are not always 'straight and narrow', are you?!"

"I don't know what you mean…" Hilary gave her 'befuddled professor' impression that was easily conjured up when she knew someone was right, but Hilary did not want to admit it.

"Charles. What's going on there?"

"Nothing, really. He still pops in from time to time, which is fine. We are like old friends."

"Friends?"

"Anna is also pregnant."

Fliss's expression turned solemn. "Hilary, I am so sorry. You never mentioned that in your letters – mind you, you could condense the Bible into a pamphlet. It must have been hell for you – finding out."

"Not at all, and don't be sorry. From the moment I first met Charles – as a teenager – I knew he was weak. The droopy dog learned how to wear the garrulous façade of 'IBM Tony'. However, underneath that act his very courteous but vacillating personality remained intact."

"You loved him..."

"Perhaps, and maybe I still do, because he is good for me, and at the time he reappeared in 'Tony' guise, he was exactly what I needed."

"But it sounds like there is a gap that someone else could squeeze through. So, Hilary – will that person be male... or female?"

"Clever question! The answer is in the future, and we haven't reached that place yet."

"We never reach it – we just keep trying to hunt it down. An eternal odyssey."

"Fliss, you always want to know what is going to happen next, don't you? I believe that whether the people in a relationship are 'straight and narrow', gay, black, white, with or without a disability, it is the quality of their love, the adhesive strength of their glue, that matters. That is what I would want to 'happen next', *if* I meet the person you term as 'the right one'! Anyway – leaving the philosophy aside, I have put deckchairs in the garden, so what would you like to drink? A martini mixer?"

"Just juice, please." Fliss patted her bump. "I don't drink or smoke anymore and... I am no longer a reckless driver!"

They toured the garden while Hilary updated Fliss on her bourgeoning career. "I am involved in a complete modernisation of the county library's school services, particularly targeted to what pupils will find on the shelves, both at school and in the general libraries. Technology is moving forward faster than anyone could have anticipated, yet there are few books to inform or reflect on digital innovation. In addition, there are whole areas of the curriculum that retain many textbooks which belong in the pre-war era. I am loving it. At last girls and boys will have resources fitting to current times, developments and discoveries. I have a team of staff to manage, so I do not have space in my life for a hot-blooded or formal liaison – with anyone."

Hilary and Fliss sank into the deckchairs.

"Well done, Hilary – that is impressive. But you have friends, other than Charles?"

"Oh yes. Sandra, a couple of others… I see Ruth quite often. She is pregnant again."

"I often think of our friendship, Hilary; it is so durable despite our vastly different characters. True friends are rafts that carry us from one experience – one shore – to another on this voyage of life. I guess that you and Ruth took it in turns to be rafts upon the waves of Thistle's death."

"You were also a raft; the one that crossed the English Channel."

"Do you think about her very often – Thistle?"

Hilary sipped her juice and admired the rockery, now a topsy-turvy scattering of animated alpines and gleeful ground cover.

"Yes. I do. Thistle grows here in my garden, amongst its floral offspring, as well as in the long grass, but I don't mind that. The garden is a manifestation of an untainted, blameless Thistle. She was never sturdy enough to be a raft of true friendship, but she could be a squall wind between shores. Without having known her would we have made our journeys? Even if at the time we chose to sail over unexpected waters?"

"A catalyst for change... talking of cats... who are they?"

At that moment two short-haired tortoiseshell felines darted out from under the rear boundary shrubs, made a beeline for Hilary and rubbed themselves around her calves. "Meet 'Nature' and 'Nurture', brother and sister – rescue cats. They weren't very old, so I was able to rename them."

"Ha – still the rescuer! They match your glasses; I am glad you didn't switch to metal frames. But why those names for them?"

"Because they remind me of questions I have about Thistle. How much of her character was inherently in her nature, and how much sprouted from the nurturing of which she had so little. Do you know that if you put a seed potato in a dark place, it will grow towards the source of any light? If that light is only available through a narrow crack it will arch and expand its flesh in that direction, but the result is a misshapen vegetable."

"Hilary, you still soak up quirky facts, don't you?" Fliss smiled at her with affection and continued, "When we asked Thistle's dad about her personality as a small child, he said she was sweet and caring. So, it must have been her upbringing."

"He betrayed her in life – he wasn't going to do the same in death. He evidenced a temper, and her mother seems to have had no empathy or conscience. Thistle could have inherited those traits."

"True, but my money is on the nurturing. My parents' love came naturally. There was plenty of scope for it to fail but it didn't. Like a source of spring water, it continued to shower down on me."

Hilary sighed. "Whereas the parental guidance, regard and interaction that I received was in the main pretty abysmal. However, the original parenting that Thistle was subject to was tenuous and potentially damaging. From eight years old it was virtually non-existent, bar a few years with foster parents. Yet she could love the keys of a piano, and the plant life all around her."

"Those were the loves that the foster parents nurtured in her, but even that story wasn't to have a happy ending."

"There is also another contributory factor in all of this…"

"You mean what happened to her as a little girl?"

"I don't know whether Thistle ever recalled the detail, she may have blanked it out of her mind, but I believe she wore the vulgarity of it like a mill-stone around her neck. I remember her being uneasy about her body and she always kept it unnaturally thin – like a boy's. Was that foul invasion of her childhood purity an additional weight that pulled her down until she drowned in drugs and alcohol? It's just supposition, but Mick couldn't hold her head above water, though I am sure he tried his best to."

"Did he move away?"

"So I heard."

Hilary disappeared to feed the cats.

On her return Fliss declared, "If I had two cats, I would name them 'Destiny' and 'Chance'. Was I destined to meet Mat – was it written in the stars? Or was it just a fortuitous throw of the dice? When you and I went up to the Anchor Inn to celebrate your twenty-fifth birthday, was it fated to be a Saturday evening – Thistle's stint? Or just a one in seven chance? Is our parentage pre-determined or also 'luck of the draw'?"

"If so, I drew a short straw." Hilary stuck out her tongue.

"And I have had another thought."

"Crikey – are you feeling well? All this 'thinking' nowadays. Is that what pregnancy does?"

"I wish more people knew how dry your humour can be, Hilary! The thought was, what if our personality originates from the circumstances of our conception? I was conceived through my parents' love for each other. They planned to have me and wanted me. Just as my own baby is. Mat and I didn't want to wait – I am already twenty-seven. We would like to have more than one child, and while we are young enough to take an active part in their growing up. Also, I don't want us to rapidly become a burden, like your parents have. Thistle's dad admitted that he had taken advantage of her mother. Thistle was not born of love – that might explain why she couldn't show it."

"Interesting. You have obviously widened your reading to more than trashy novels! But I do not envisage that you would ever become a 'burden' on anyone; you are too lovely."

"Ummm, I am about *not* to be 'lovely'."

"Go on."

"In this theory of mine, I am having enormous difficulty imagining your parents at the moment of your conception…"

Hilary pulled the most austere of her 'unimpressed librarian' expressions.

Fliss curled up her lips into the smirk for which she was perennially famous, that little did she know was about to be passed on to her next generation.